# Dementia
## A Novella

### by

### Hans Peter Braendlin

*Dementia*

Published by Biblio Publishing
The Educational Publisher, Inc.
1313 Chesapeake Ave
Columbus, OH 43004
www.BiblioPublishing.com
ISBN: 978-1-62249-061-5
Library of Congress Catalog Number: 2013943649

In memoriam
Trudy

*T*hey found Nurse on the pavement early this morning, Jonathan says. Her neck broken and her head smashed in. Right under Gloria's window four stories above. You went to Gloria's room last night. You remember. The window was open. You watched Gloria sleep. Peaceful...

Rock-a-bye Baby...

Then *she* came...

What are you doing here? Why are you standing? Where's your wheelchair? Get out of here! Now! You have no business here, you old lech. And the doctors will know pronto you can walk. What a fraud!...

She shouldn't have...

Always telling you what to do...

Rearranging things—deranging—the tables, the chairs, the vases, the photos, although she knows you like your things a certain way, your way, in their certain places...

You know she took the watch Marlene had given you...

Getting you up at night, when it's her night shift. We don't want to wet the bed, do we... Hut two three four!... Making you get up even though you don't have to go, even though you can control yourself, and she knows it...

\*\*\*\*

Taking the pipe tobacco away, saying it's poison. Saying you can't smoke on the balcony either. Locking the Glenlivet away, saying it's poison. Telling Edie to stop bringing that stuff—the tobacco and the Scotch—though the flowers are okay...

Jonathan says detectives are here, looking around and talking to the doctors, the staff, and some of the residents. The investigation would go on, but for the time being they had to take precautionary measures. You were in the hall—nailed to the ground, you and your wheelchair—when they came, the white smocks, pulling Gloria, struggling and crying, to the elevator—one of those between the women's side and the men's side of the floor—to the elevator going down. Why me? What have I done? Not to the tombs! No! Please, please, don't take me *there*! No!...

That shouldn't have happened...

Gloria had told you the tombs are what the other residents here call the rooms in the basement, where the doors are always locked from the outside, where the windows are small and high up, just above the ground level outside, and have bars on them—I think she said they have bars—where they have a little garden only, with a high fence around it, not open and free like the big garden she and I like so much—The tombs are where they keep you from wandering away, or from hurting yourself, where they keep you when they think you might hurt somebody else...

They shouldn't do that to Gloria...

Nurse... All because of *her*...

You must do something... Think of something...

Nurse has a name, but I've forgotten it. Must ask Jonathan to tell me again, next time he comes by...

****

I don't forget Jonathan's name. He finds my tobacco and holds

it for safekeeping. He lets me smoke on the balcony, even inside
when the windows are open. He says I cured his father's cancer.
James. James Sawtelle. That was a long time ago, but I
remember. Pancreatic. We caught it in time.

I can remember the past. At times.

I need to. Now more than ever.

Mustn't let the now make me forget...

Many things to think of—earlier things, elsewhere—the good
and the bad. Rethinking them, getting a grasp on them. Being
there...

When I'm here it's difficult. Here I forget things...

Jonathan finds the Glenlivet. He knows it helps me remember.
Smoking the pipe does too.
...

Is *that* why Nurse...?

Jonathan, he's different. He tells Edie to go on bringing the
tobacco and the Scotch...

He found the watch—when was that?—he found it way back in
the drawer of the night-stand, under some papers...

\*\*\*\*

I want it to be him who helps me get dressed. He's patient.
Unlike Nurse. He comes and gets me, often. Talks to me.
Listens to me. Pushes the wheelchair, to the garden, or to the
salon next to the dining hall. When we're not in the garden—
when the weather is bad—Gloria and I like to be in the salon

before lunch and dinner and in the afternoons...

They don't know I could do all that by myself—get dressed, get into the wheelchair, maneuver it. They don't know I actually don't need a wheelchair. I keep that to myself—for the time being, until I find my bearings—keep it even from Jonathan and Edie. Except Edie knows I can handle the chair.

Gloria knows I can walk. That's how I get to her room. I walk. What luck we're on the same floor! I walk from the men's side of the floor to the women's side—When nobody's around...

Making sure first it's evening...

It's hard to keep track of time here, in this place...

Ring the bell, Nurse says...

On Jonathan's days off it can happen that nobody pays any attention to me... It can happen that nobody comes to get me for lunch or dinner. Ring the bell, she says. Ring when?...

What *is* this place?...

If it weren't for Gloria—and Jonathan—I'd get the hell out of here…

Why lunch at eleven and dinner at five-thirty?... Who eats at those times?...

I don't like the dining hall. I'm uncomfortable among a crowd of people, but it's more than that, isn't it. It's as if everybody's waiting for something, waiting, not knowing what for... Makes me feel clammy...

\*\*\*\*

Worse, I can't sit with Gloria. Michael—calls himself the maitre d'—says I can't. Gloria's table and mine are fully occupied. No room for additional seating. No exchanges either. The residents like to keep the same seat assignments, he says. It makes them feel at home. And because most of them have their own wine, water, or soda bottles, or are on special diets, they have to stay put—That's what he said, they *have* to stay put— with nameplates by their place settings to remind them where they belong—Hut! Hut! But if there's a departure from one of our tables—He said departure, didn't he?—he'll see to it that an arrangement is made!... Ninety-nine bottles of beer on the wall... More likely ninety-nine *luftballons*, waiting to drift away... Marlene loved that song... Carl, your mind's wandering. Get a hold of yourself!...

I think he's full of it. I want to sit with Gloria right away—don't want to wait. Must talk to him again. More forcefully...

I could have lunch and dinner in my bedroom, at that little table, where I have breakfast. But then I wouldn't see Gloria. Maybe I couldn't even sit with her before the meals, in the garden or in the salon. I wouldn't like that at all. The dining hall it is. At least I can *look* at her there...

The people at my table. Next to me that dapper guy, jacket and tie all the time, big, strong looking, but not always clean. His room on the same floor as mine, I think. Didn't I see him in the hall once? I *think* it's the same man. I forgot what his nameplate says. Likes to joke a lot. His laugh the bleat of a goat. Smells like one, too. Incontinence? Maybe *he* should have all his meals in his room... His seat would become free...

\*\*\*\*

Opposite me that woman—Don't know her name—Tall, bony, pointy nose, all that makeup. Looks like the Witch of the West.

5

A mole on the ridge of her nose—like a third eye, it's so big. Talking a lot—I don't remember what about. Gives me the glad eye all the time. Those incisors, an inch long it seems. You want to cross your legs when you see her bite into food. That time when her foot touched mine, inadvertently I thought, but then it happened twice again—I now keep my feet under my chair...

You're being uncharitable, downright unkind—What is it with you?...

Next to her that shriveled-up old fellow—Don't know *his* name either—Doesn't look well, chin on his chest all the time, eyes on the plate, doesn't speak. Has difficulties pushing his dentures back in when they fall out. A nasty cough, repeatedly. A candidate for imminent departure?...

Now *that*, Carl, that's ugly...

Why do I feel so uneasy today, so tight?...

It had been so good with Gloria...

Have to get up from the wheelchair... Up!... That's it... Walk around a little...

The mirror—it hangs crooked... You gave it to Marlene when we were in Venice... Have to adjust it...

**** 

That man there, Carl, in the mirror, he doesn't look all that old. It's his baby skin, Edie keeps telling him. Dad's skin. It's the sparkle in his eyes, Gloria says. She knows he can walk. He can do that—and *then* some, thanks to her. It's their secret. Theirs only, again, now that Nurse...

Some time ago—Carl forgot when—Gloria had sat down on a bench next to his chair, in the garden, by the bushes with the red flowers, the bushes next to those with the yellow flowers— Jonathan had placed him there, after Edie had gone home, leaving him with his pipe and tobacco. I'm Gloria. I'm Carlton. Carl. She's beautiful. Makes me feel young. Cuts through the fog here. She's dainty, like a daffodil. Delicate features. Expressive hands—hands of an artist. That slightly crooked smile, dynamite. The lips full and soft, sweetly curved. They made him want to kiss them. Wrinkles, but they look good, make her look good, and strong—Character! White hair, totally white. Wavy, down to the shoulders—gorgeous. Those deep blue eyes, luminous, warm. Sometimes a faraway look in them.

They had talked. Carl doesn't remember what about, except that it was good, that it was warm. Again the days after that. In the garden, or in the salon next to the dining hall, before the meals, which he likes too when Gloria's with him, when it doesn't matter that he can't smoke there. He doesn't remember what they talked about. Except for the time when it wasn't good, when it was cold, when she said she may have to do chemo. Breast cancer. His hand had hurt from the clenching of the fist...

Must ask Jonathan about that—Have they done all the tests, all the scans, radiation, explored all the possibilities?...

Her smiling that crooked smile, I'll turn bald.

****

Then the day when she said come I'll take you to my room. It's more comfortable there. She told Jonathan she'd see to me— she'd push my chair.

They had looked at her photo album. This is Frank my husband. This is Frank Junior. They're dead, died together twelve years

7

ago, in a car crash. Carl had told her his wife Marlene had also died in a car accident, and his daughter Jo was dead as well. He hadn't told her he had been driving the car, and how Jo died. Gloria had taken his hand and given it a squeeze.

Taking me to her room again the following evening, after dinner. Standing there, silhouetted against the light of the setting sun, smiling at me. The aureole! Why do I remember *that* so clearly? As clearly as I remember the past? She's so beautiful...

****

Carl gets off the wheelchair and walks to her. She looks surprised, then laughs. She cups his face with her hands, pulls his head down to hers, kisses him. First softly. Then hard, her mouth open, her tongue seeking his. She unbuttons his shirt and slides it off. She moves his hand to the top button of her blouse. He unbuttons the blouse and slides it off. No bra. She takes his hands and places them on her breasts. Small, but still round and firm, wondrously. He strokes them, gently. She laughs, a laugh of pleasure. She opens the belt of his pants, unzips them, pulls them down, then his shorts. He steps out of them. She places a hand on his genitals, strokes him, gently. He feels the stiffening, implausible as it seems. She laughs, delightedly, and pulls him to her. He kisses her. Hard, wet. She drops her skirt, her panties, steps out of them and her shoes. She takes his hand and places it between her legs. Wondrously soft, wet, warm. She takes him by the hand and leads him to the bed, placing him down on it...

The passion had come, out of the past it had seemed. Slowly and gently at first, then rapidly, fiercely, intensely, all senses afire with power—silencing the pain of the past...

Carl still had his shoes and socks on, he had suddenly been aware of, had not been aware of before.

You had walked to her room the following night, and again last night. She had fallen asleep afterwards.

Then *she* had come...

You can't let them keep Gloria in the tombs. Must talk to them...

The fog again—with her down there now—the fog taking hold of me again...

Carl! Do you have a moment?

Jonathan. With a man. Didn't hear them enter.

This is Detective Pierce. He would like to talk to you.

A detective? What's *this* about?

Detective Pierce. How do you do? Please have a seat.

Thank you, Mister Carothers. But this won't take long. I just have a question or two. About Nurse Critch.

Critch! Of course! Martha Critch. That's her name. You remember now.

What about her?

Last night—Have you seen or heard anything unusual?

Not a thing.

I understand you're friends with Gloria Marlowe.

Marlowe! You forgot her last name is Marlowe! Why does this

happen to you?... But that other thing, about you being friends with Gloria, that's a good one... If only he knew.

Yes, we're friends.

When you talked to her, did she reveal any animosity toward Nurse Critch?

What's going on here? What gives with this animosity thing? Gloria a suspect? Are they nuts?

Not Gloria. No way.

Now, *you* and Nurse, that's another matter, but he doesn't need to know that.

So you agree with the people here who say she's a very gentle person, non-violent?

Gentle? Ha! You want to shout it to the world that she can be aggressive—beautifully, sublimely aggressive. But the world mustn't know. Not yet anyway.

Gloria gentle? Absolutely. She wouldn't hurt a fly.

And now, Mister Carothers, I have to ask, can you account for your activities last night and early this morning?

Aha! *Your* turn now. Your activities? Wouldn't he like to know... Gloria!... But what happened afterwards, when you were about to leave? It's all in a haze... Something with Nurse... Whatever... He mustn't know you were there.

I was here. The TV, then sleeping.

Thank you. I have no further questions for now. But I may want to talk to you again at a later time.

Push the chair toward him. Make it seem difficult. Give him a limp hand to shake.

I'll be here. Where else would I go?

He and Jonathan are leaving. Jonathan's waving at me, smiling...

You've got to do something about Gloria... Get going... Clear the fog...

Sort things out first...

That photo, there, the one of him of the hard eyes, staring at you from within his baby skin, and of the woman who would never be your mother, whom you never knew. You killed her, he said to you when you were five, Edie nine. Edie said our mother died giving birth to you. But it's not your fault. How come it's my fault, you asked him. You were big and caused complications, he said. What does complications mean, you remember asking. You demanded too much of her, took too much away from her. You took her away from me. It's unjust. You must bear the responsibility. What does responsibility mean, you asked. You'll know some day, he said.

You've been sharply attuned to complications, injustices, responsibility ever since.

He did a lot for him, Edie had tried to convince him. No money spared. All those expensive toys, the stereo system. Tennis lessons—on the private court. The fitness room just for him. Only the very best in clothes. All those nannies. Only the very best private schools. The camps, two every summer. Columbia...

Columbia was good. The world opened itself. The classes, and Carlo and Charles, Caroline—they were the first ones to call me Carl—we were the four Charleys...

\*\*\*\*

Before that, no. The world was closed. Despite Edie. She was away all that time, at the boarding schools. Why didn't he send Carl to boarding schools too, instead of those academies in the city? He ran away once, but the police caught him. After that just waiting, waiting to get away... Why keep him next to him but distant and cold, looking at him with the hurtful hurt in his eyes, when they weren't hard, having breakfast by himself, going to his study upstairs right away after supper, leaving him alone, again, alone with the nannies—whose faces and names he has forgotten—then alone with the housekeepers—he remembers the last seven—or is it eight?—Gracie, then Pearl, then Jodie, then Marge, then Sun Lin, then Mary, then Concepcion—Concepcion!—then Elizabeth?

\*\*\*\*

He was a stranger in his father's house. Kept in the nest to suffer estrangement in it. The motherless nest. The fatherless nest. It was easy to fly away when the time came. It was agonizing at first to have flown away. Had you tried hard enough to engage him? Do or say something that was warm and close enough? But then the memories of the isolation, the loneliness, that came back on those visits home. Then those lectures on what to aim for in life when he came down from his study... Calling me a bleeding heart for going to Med School instead of Business School... The condescension. The intransigence. The fog. Which gave sharp clarity to the world of difference between the closed world and the open world.

Put the photo down—put it face down... There!

\*\*\*\*

You said no when he wanted to move in with you. With Marlene and Jo gone, he said, you have the space and the time to take care of me. Take care of the cancer that's eating me up. Which cancer, you wanted to ask. Carlton can't take care of you by himself, Edie said. You need to be in a hospital or a nursing home. He raised a hand, waving her off. He can do it, he said. It's his responsibility. He's a cancer specialist after all, and I paid for much of his education. Listen to Edie, you said, you really need proper care, with the necessary equipment, and nurses to look after you all the time. He looked at you, looked at you with that hurtful hurt in his eyes. Now you want to kill your father too.

Today's my seventh day here, Jonathan says. What's seven days? Here and now? I sometimes know time, but it's the earlier time, the time before now. The now time, that's hard. I know space, know some of the space even here. My rooms. The hall. The elevators. The salon and the dining hall. The garden. But I find it hard to orient myself here—except in Gloria's room.

Why do the walls here seem so close at times?...

I need to take care of my rooms. Things have to be in their places, where they belong. It helps me to belong to myself here—sort of. It helps me now and then to remember the here of now. Nurse, but also the cleaning women—Why do I forget their names too?—It's not like me—they keep shifting things, and I have to see to it right away that they're in the right places.

The bathroom. Make sure I have the toothbrush in the first glass, there, the toothpaste in the second, my skin cream and deodorant close to the right of the sink, my electric razor, my comb and hairbrush next to them. Make sure I have my bar of soap in the shower stall. Can't stand that liquid stuff.

The things have to be in their places.

****

The bedroom. Adjust the bed to its proper height again. They don't do it right. Push the night-stand closer to the bed. They leave too much space in-between, and I can't reach the switch on the lamp unless I get up... You don't need any light after we put you to bed, she says...

Their wall closet, where they keep my clothes, bed sheets, towels, that stuff—three doors, the one in the middle always locked. No key—Nurse—she hides the Glenlivet and the tobacco there. Ha! No matter. Jonathan gets them for me.

I like that little table by the window, where I have breakfast. I like to sit facing the window. To see the garden, the trees. Jonathan puts the tray down where I want it. Nurse puts it down where I have to face their little TV in the corner. You don't need to look outside, she says. Too bright—bad for your eyes. She turns the set on, to the news on that weird station, the zombie station—dead souls speaking—where the news is not news but pronouncements of soul-less opinions... Why does she try so hard to get to me?... I walk to the TV and turn it off after she leaves and place the wheelchair and tray where I want them. She doesn't know I do this, doesn't know I can. Somebody else—a cleaning woman—comes and gets the tray. On the days I have the tobacco for my pipe, on Jonathan's days, I open the window and have a smoke with the last two cups of coffee. I don't think of anything in particular, at breakfast. I like that. I just look at the garden and the trees outside. It's nice and bright outside.

****

Marlene's paintings, the two I have in the bedroom—the other two are in the living room. The strongest four of the oils she left behind, four of those that made her even more famous, works with especially bold and hard strokes, primary colors, mainly, and blacks and whites, aggressive, paintings of people dying—hunger, diseases, murders, car crashes—of people in despair—hunger, diseases, fear, souls in torment—images of violence and pain that had taken hold of her mind with special fury, had haunted her without mercy—paintings she did when she had been drinking a lot again, thinking again of the son born still because of the drinking... Nurse says they're inhuman and she'll see to it I get pictures of the Madonna and baby Jesus, and of Christ on the cross. They have plenty of them stored in the basement, also a Saint Sebastian or two. The slings and arrows of outrageous fortune...

Through the open archway the living room... The things here are all mine. That helps. Jonathan says Edie insisted that they let me have them right away.

The teak bookcase, stained black—the last piece Jo had made—the bookcase with the many albums in it and some of the books I used to like, don't, can't, read anymore—can't concentrate—with the side compartment where I keep the Scotch glasses and where Jonathan puts the Glenlivet, after rescuing it from the closet.

****

On top of the bookcase the photos, there, and the vases, the little silver one and the big one in glass. Edie's flowers in them.

The TV—I like its black frame—Edie had given it to me when I was alone in the house, rattling around in it... How many years?...

The two easy chairs Marlene had found in that antique shop—

two years before she died, wasn't it? Or was it three? The wood stained black, the upholstery beige.

The two little black coffee tables Jo had made, had made all by herself when she was seventeen, when all was still well.

On the walls Marlene's other two paintings—Strange how soothing their violence—and the Venetian mirror I had given her.

Above the bookcase the sarong, mounted, framed black, with threads of gold woven into the fabric—the sarong which the Sultan of Brunei had given to the woman who couldn't be a mother to Edie and me... The oil company, of which he eventually became the chairman, had seen to it that the government sent him as a cultural attaché—cultural!—to oil-rich Brunei, the faraway land where I was born, where our mother died... I kept the sarong because *she* had worn it—she, the stranger to memory, elsewhere, outside, way outside, but wanting to come in...

****

It helps having my things here, in place here, seeing to it they're in order, everything neatly in place.

They look back at you, saying, remember...

They found Carl lying on the kitchen floor, Jonathan says. Filthy, unkempt, having neglected himself, disoriented, incoherent. A week's need of medications, untouched, lying on the kitchen counter. The sink full of dirty dishes and pans. The neighbors had seen the windows shuttered for three days, upstairs and downstairs, had called Edie, who had called for an ambulance. They had taken him to Geriatrics—in the hospital—Jonathan says, and two days later he was taken from there to this place. Carl only remembers arriving here, and from then on—now and then.

****

That first day. He remembers. The doctor said he was almost fine, physically, except that he was undernourished and weak, and he had problems with walking because the blood pressure was way too low. Not enough blood going to the legs, also the arms. They'd give him a wheelchair and have people push him until he was stronger and could handle it himself. But mainly it was the mind. Not always clear. Keeps shifting things. He wasn't laying down memory at times. Short-term memory losses. What the fuck? Isabel hadn't told you *that*. Or had she? You should have suspected. The difficulties you had, increasingly, with the phone, names, shopping, cooking, cleaning up. The doctor—Carl forgot his name—had added he'd continue taking the meds his physician—that's Isabel— had prescribed...

Nurse had been present—I remember that too. Had talked to me in baby language. My, we're cute, those large hazel eyes, that soft white hair—though we'll need to wash and comb it often, won't we—Strong little hands, and we're such a trim and tall boy. But now we go beddy-bye and have sweet dreams.

Her language was different after that, when nobody else was present. But the following day it had been Jonathan. And the day after that, I think, my things had been here. Edie!

Edie had given Carl that big TV, with HD, DVR, and all that. He remembers she wouldn't let him pay for it. It was a precious gift because she could hardly afford it, Bill having died—Edie having earlier lost Carlton and Christine—How strong she is, Edie!—Carlton, whom she named after our father and me, Carlton has been dead for many years now. Then Christine dying, ovarian cancer, suddenly, metastasizing voraciously. You couldn't help even though you threw everything at her, and Christine's twins— Joanna and Joellen I think their names are—live with Edie now. That's why Edie can only stay till two when she comes to see me, because she has to be there when the girls come home from school. She's come to see me almost every day, I think, after lunch, from twelve till two. Didn't she say once she'd come some time soon on a Saturday or Sunday, with the twins?—And she said something about a birthday.

\*\*\*\*

She likes Gloria... Once, before she went home, she came down with me to the garden, to meet Gloria. I don't remember what we talked about, except that it was nice...

Edie and I are close...

The TV screen is huge. That's him, that man there in the wheelchair, Carl, in the reflection. Edie sometimes turns the set on. He tries to watch the animal shows he had grown to like at home. Or a nature or culture show. The Alps, the Forum of Rome, the Steppes of Russia, the columns of Ephesus. Sometimes Stewart and Colbert, which Jonathan had taped. Carl can't do that by himself. Nurse refuses, saying they're snakes in the grass and socialists... *He* would have liked her...

It's difficult watching TV, here. Carl can't focus. You catch him pushing the wheelchair back, around, forward, back again. What should he do now? What's this about? What's he doing here?... That time, some days ago, when Edie—Why were her eyes so large and moist?—when she said, come, let's look at a photo album. Your travels. Remember your travels?

I took those trips after Jo died, took pictures—I do remember that, don't I—Tanzania, of course, twice, China, Japan, India,

Mexico, Guatemala, Peru, the Philippines, Australia, Papua New Guinea—I still know geography?—Other countries, Brazil and Argentina as well... Brunei—Brunei twice too...

Taking those trips as often as possible...

Carl sometimes looks at an album with Edie, but more often he says no. He can't focus. He would like to go down to the garden—maybe.

Why is the photo of him and our would-be mother face down? Nurse! Must place it upright... There!... I like to look at *her*. The resemblance to Edie when she was young. Beautiful, elegant. Fine features, long blond hair—glowing—deep blue eyes, looking straight at me, with a faint, faraway smile in them. Who was she? How did she look in the sarong? Who would she have been? How would *he* have been with her still by his side?...

There the photos of Marlene and Jo, next to each other.

Marlene... She wanted to drive. You didn't let her. She had had too much at the party.

The fog. Watch out! The truck, suddenly...

Jo... The blood spattered on the wall. The teeth embedded in it.

Men shoot themselves, the police detective said. Women jump off bridges, or such. Women don't shoot themselves. Certainly not in the mouth...

You killed him for that—Leonard...

But you too were responsible...

I can't deal with that right now.

****

The flowers. That's better right now. Edie knows I like simple flowers—daisies, daffodils, day lilies, whatever she can find—forget-me-nots too. There the daffodils, and there the forget-me-nots. She brought them yesterday—I think it was yesterday. The colors. Dainty and modest, but rich when Carl looks closely, bending down to them. The faint, discreet smell. The innocence, childlike, captivating...

Daddy, catch me!

She liked to take a running leap into my arms...

No!... That's not better right now.

The little silver vase—delicate... She had given it to me when she was nine, a lifetime ago. Had bought it with her allowance...

This is bad too. You don't want to think of it now.

The big vase, Murano glass, Carlo's gift to Marlene and me. Had brought it on a visit back to the States—His grandparents had grown up in Venice, before moving to Bologna, then escaping the Fascists—Carlo had told Marlene and me we should see Venice, after visiting Giulia and him in Rome. Which we did... It was good, and then not, as it turned out... The mirror—You bought it for Marlene, as a surprise for her birthday. She loved it.

The Murano vase, Carlo's gift, with dark and light greens, mainly, and bright yellows and reds here and there, insistent, reminding him of the colors outside—the trees, the bushes, the yellow and red flowers.

****

Go and look outside!... There!

Now further beyond, more distant! The spaces, the moments and stretches in time, beyond the here and now of the garden and the trees. Be there. Rethink things, how and why things happened. Remembering the beauty, the violence, the good and the bad... Try to make sense of it all... Must come to terms, find peace of mind... Gloria...

Clarity!...

Carlo. Carlo Bandetti. We called him the Bandit. Restless Carlo. He loved his Alfa Romeo, second-hand, which he tinkered with, souped up, raced on the Interstate, bringing home speeding tickets... Years later—he was forty-five—racing another speedster, on another Interstate, the Autostrada. Jumped the median, met an oncoming semi.

He had been high on rage at the world, Giulia said at the funeral.

The manner of his death was appropriate, the way it punctuated his life, his explosive and high-speed energy...

**\*\*\*\***

Carlo, my dorm-mate at Columbia for two years, before we rented that two-bedroom apartment together with Charles—another dear friend... Him too losing his life so early, when he was thirty-five, losing it to hate... Then Caroline in the apartment as well, Caroline, much more than a friend, who died when she was twenty-five, her body found on a shore of the Black Sea—Caroline, driven to liberate women from sexual slavery... What should you have done to prevent her from going? What could you have done?
...

Carlo loved to party. Tried to introduce you to drinking, but you didn't like it, then. Your father drank, a lot, drank in his study. All those empty bottles in the waste. Alcohol made me sick to the stomach, made me throw up. What a shame, Carlo said, it's fun to get wasted now and then... What a waste his life, ending the way it did, though it was anger that intoxicated him then.

Having people over, usually on the weekends, women too, late into the night. Drinking—Well, sodas for me, then—and dancing. Carlo a terrific dancer, sinewy, sensuous, liberating. The women adored him, the lithe body, the curly black hair, the dark brown eyes—alert and humorous—the sharp wit, the uninhibited, engaging laugh.

Carlo often not alone in his bed. The Bandit there as well. Women adored him. You don't mind, do you? I didn't, even though the noises of passion and pleasure kept me awake sometimes. I liked him too much.

Him wanting you to have sex too. Are you a virgin? Are you averse to sex? Keeping yourself for the right woman? Do you prefer men? He later knew I wasn't averse to sex, with a woman, when Caroline came to stay—Caroline, sweet and gentle, but fierce in her fight against the abuse of women. She returned your love for her, you're sure, but did you abuse it? Were you too possessive? Not possessive enough? Was any of it why, how, you failed her, even though she said you didn't? ...

Failing Marlene... and Jo.

Gloria. Carl mustn't fail *her*, not her too... She's the good that's coming your way now... You remember last night, the way she embraced you, holding you tight afterwards...

Concepcion.

You weren't a virgin, before Caroline. Not exactly.

You knew your father had each of the women, those he hired to take care of the house and you, as a bed-mate now and then. You saw them go to his room, you heard the noises. Bodies to be used—He called people of color darkies, wetbacks, or slant-eyes, but it must not have mattered to him what color of skin they had when they were in his bed. As long as they serviced him and otherwise kept out of his way—Gracie, then Pearl, then Jodie, then Marge, then Sun Lin, then Mary, then Concepcion, then Elizabeth. Mary letting it slip once that he paid a very good salary, plus bonuses. But they all came and went. Did he discard them when he tired of them?

Not Concepcion. He fired *her* when he found out about her and you.

\*\*\*\*

You were sixteen.

Concepcion, petite, fragile, long black hair, usually in braids, lightly brown soft skin, soft brown almond-shaped eyes. *Pobrecito*, she murmured when she enfolded the boy with her arms. She had come to his room one night, in her nightgown, her hair loose and down to her waist, sliding into bed with him, just like that. Had pulled him on top of her, had guided him into her. Hadn't taught him how to make love, had just taken him into her. It had been over in less than a minute, though her arms kept enfolding him, pulling him closer, *Pobrecito*. Then another night. He got an inkling of how to please, but it was without guidance, was awkward. The third night a response, though close to being hidden and mute. A slight arching and stiffening of the body and a whimper, *Pobrecito*.

She was gone the following day.

His eyes had held that hurtful hurt, then they had turned hard. Do you know anything other than how to take?...

Gloria... Desire coming full circle in my life...

She makes you respond again to humanity, the good of it—responsibility, justice.
...

But what if you're cuckoo?...

\*\*\*\*

Carlo knowing all along he'd major in Political Science, and why. His grandfather had been a professor of Politology at the University of Bologna, was fired when the Fascists took over. Threatening phone calls. A colleague imprisoned. Former students of his beaten up. He had to flee. To avoid arrest at a border checkpoint, he left with his wife and son, Carlo's father to be, for Naples, got passage for Sardinia, bribed a man there to sail them to Corsica in the dark of night. From there to Paris, where he got visas to the States, and then from Brest by freighter to New York, where he worked for two years as a janitor, waiting for an academic job and then getting it, at Berkeley, because of his world-wide reputation. Carlo's father died early—Leukemia—when Carlo was two. His mother and he moved in with the grandparents.

Carlo learning a lot from his grandfather, building on that knowledge... From Columbia to graduate studies at NYU, then teaching Political Science at Berkeley, where he joined the students in demonstrations. Exhilarating, he said, because full of hope, still, at that time. Then driven to go into politics—Teaching and scholarship don't do it for me, he said. Going to Italy—Going home, he said, but what is home?... Marlene and he had separated by then... Carlo marrying Giulia—It was a good marriage while his life lasted—Carlo getting citizenship, getting elected, fighting the new Fascism, fighting a losing battle, he said, the erosion progressive, but one mustn't give up, one must keep the anger fierce...

\*\*\*\*

Those darkly decisive, troubled moments at NYU and in the next apartment—You too were admitted to NYU after Columbia, Caroline and Charles as well... It's all so far back now, that time at NYU, that time too... But close in the memory.

Carlo then living with Marlene, who was a student at the New York Academy of Art. Her grandparents had left Germany with their daughter, Marlene's grandfather seeing the handwriting on the wall. He taught art, was a close friend to Expressionist painters, whose works the degenerate Nazis labeled Degenerate Art, destroying much of it—Carlo's kinship with Marlene, Marlene, whom you eventually fell in love with, after Caroline was gone—Marlene who became your wife, eventually.

Carlo was happy for you...

But things were more complicated than that, weren't they. Already then...

Carl's getting ahead of himself... Mustn't stray all over the place—have to keep my memories in proper order...

\*\*\*\*

Carlo with his full scholarship to Columbia. Had straight A's, even in the first two years, had a steel-trap memory. Instead of studying, other than writing term papers, on that Olivetti of his, him listening to Italian operas, joining the tenors in their arias, sometimes the sopranos, managing to climb the register. You don't mind, do you? I didn't. He had a beautiful voice, even in fake falsetto. I was able to concentrate doing the homework, had to, but sometimes going to the library—Learning didn't come easy for you. You didn't ask Carlo for help, he didn't offer it—he understood you had to climb that hill on your own.

Those discussions with fellow students, well into the night. Talking about many things, including shows, art and art exhibits, literature, music, professors and courses, what to aim for in life, and politics. You listening, mainly, absorbing, When it was politics Carlo kept returning to the subject of Fascism, to the annoyance of some, who said he was unduly obsessed with it.

****

Let's see, what was it again, the gist of Carlo's thoughts? Something like, Fascism is very much alive. Lingering on subterraneously after Mussolini, the Nazis, Franco, then the disease surfacing again, and spreading full force, though as a new strain. The will to achieve the absolute rule of the few but now totally by means of wealth, though in the shadows—The manipulation, from the shadows, of money and through it of government. The corporations and the banks. The politics of exclusion. The loopholes, the deregulations, born of greed for more. The uniforms now not boots and obscenely boy-scoutish shirts, but suits, no less obscene in their simulation of civility. The dementia now diffuse, often by chain reaction—A butterfly flapping its wings here, causing a storm there—The violence now global, most of it hidden, but some in the open, genocide too, again, and torture. A new Fascism, a Hydra rearing its many heads, though too many don't see them or take them to be pretty flowers afield.

Him once saying, You know, we both fight cancer, you one that's eating up the body, I one that's destroying the minds and souls of those hungry for power, that cancer then proceeding with the dead souls, the zombies, eating up the bodies of others...

A knock on the door?... Quick, into the wheelchair!

Come in!

It's that guy from my table, the one who sits next to me. The goat. With that funny laugh. I think it's him. What does he want?

Hey, Carl! I thought I'd pay you a visit. We're neighbors, you know. I'm two doors down the hall from you. You may have forgotten my name. Peter. Peter Morgan.

Peter. Hi!

I owe you.

Owe me? What for?

Well, as you know I'm a leaker, a regular Sir Pissalot... A problem with my bladder... It's not nice, you know, getting old... A week ago—You had just arrived here—We met in the hall. You told me to talk to the doctors here about a brand new medicine—I forgot its name—something Latin—And what do you know, it's beginning to work!

What's he talking about? I don't remember any of this.

I'm glad it's helping.

It is. Things are much better now... Hey, you have a nice room here. Comfy... A lot of black, though—I guess you like black... Weird paintings you have... I like that sarong—where did you get it?... The mirror—Venetian, right?... Family pictures, those photos?... Nice view from the window, I bet... Let me see... Ah, yes—All those trees, and the bushes, the flowers... My room faces the street. Not nearly as pretty...

He's looking at me.

How about Nurse Critch, eh? Her falling from the window like that... Some say she was pushed...

Pushed...

They say a woman on our floor did it. I saw them take her downstairs—a slim woman, dainty—Her name escapes me—But she didn't do it—Critch was a moose—It would take someone really strong to handle *her*, or someone really angry... Don't talk ill of the dead and all that, but that one was from hell! She really got to me... Always ordering me about... Other residents too... Nasty to everyone... Getting me up four or five times when it was her night shift, instead of just letting me pee in my diapers... Calling me a pig. Saying she'd see to it I have all my meals in my room because my smell is offensive... Some called her Critch-the-Bitch, but that doesn't come close... Thinking she runs this place... Those boots she wore all the time with that uniform of hers... I think she wasn't quite right upstairs, if you know what I mean... And they treat us as if *we*'re the loony ones here... Well, she's gone now...

I want to go back to the window.

You have things on your mind, I can tell—Okay, I'm off. It was nice talking to you... Let's do it again. Have a chat. Come visit *me* some time... I don't get visitors—You're really on the scrapheap when you land in this place... It can get lonely... You try to laugh it away, but...

I'll do that—Look you up, have a chat.

A bright smile.

That would be great.

**\*\*\*\***

Carl hears himself saying, Take care!...

He's gone...

Back to the window!...

Charles.

You met him in that Physics class, second semester. An option for the science part in their Liberal Studies program... Got me going in the sciences, three years later the degree in Chemistry and Biological Sciences, then Med School... Charles, that athletic body—Football in high school, running back—Deep sonorous voice, robust like his body, crinkly black hair, gleaming teeth, large dark brown eyes. Charles quiet and serious most of the time. Driven, like Carlo, but the energy held in, anger burning deep down. A mind as sharp as a tack, like Carlo's. And like Carlo, him knowing from the beginning what he wanted. Be a lawyer, a criminal defense lawyer, defending fellow Blacks, those who are part of the other in society, with different skin colors, whom society disenfranchises with pervasive virulence. *That* cancer, born from people with demented minds, the derangement killing their souls, and the dead souls eating at the lives of those others.

Charles once joking about his surname, White, saying it made him schizophrenic, but good at chess when he was given the black pieces. His father, Winston, a hard-hat, construction worker, but periodic only, frequently laid off. A quiet, sometimes brooding man, but gentle. Charles' mother, Charlene, a clerk at the DMV. A huge woman, of a vast, captivating sweetness. That one-bedroom apartment, Lower East Side. Charles sleeping on the sofa sleeper in the living room, before we had the apartment. Charlene serving soul food once, which I didn't like at all. She could tell. She laughed. Regular food for you from now on. A magnificent voice, singing Mahalia Jackson songs, and arias from Italian operas, joking about the fat lady singing. They sometimes had Carlo and Caroline over as well—later also Marlene and of course Jolene—and Charlene and Carlo sang duets together, from *Aida*, *Tosca*, *La Traviata*, *La Bohème*, other *La*'s. They had a rapt audience...

*She* sang. Edie remembers. Lullabies, other soft airs...

You're straying again...

Charles too with a scholarship—academic, not football—but a partial one only, and he had to make money, working in the evenings, sometimes into the night. This and that in the first two years, bagging, janitorial work, and such.

\*\*\*\*

That incident, early in our third year at Columbia, just after he, Carlo, and I rented the apartment. The job as a cashier at a grocery store. Arrested for stealing, supposedly a large amount over time. Beaten up at the interrogation—had his right hand broken—when he didn't confess, but being eventually allowed to make that one phone call, calling Carlo and you. You hiring a lawyer, putting your father's money to really good use—His eyes would have turned to ice had he known. The lawyer having an X-ray taken of the hand right after bail, suing the policemen involved, suing the grocery store for libel, for failing to produce evidence. The charges were dropped, Charles' record kept clean.

Him saying it was a good first-hand experience, an intimate body experience, of how many of the Brothers and other others are treated. It reinforced his determination.

While in law school clerking for a law firm, first doing the files, then research. After three years admitted to the Bar, passing the exam with flying colors. Then Public Defender, then the private practice...

The door *again*?

Have you seen Poopsie? I *have* to find her!

A guy... Naked, almost, wearing briefs only, a powerful body... Disheveled, stringy gray hair all over the face. A wild look in his eyes, what you can see of them... Where did *he* escape from?

She got away from me. Have you seen her? A Chihuahua. My little Poopsie.

Not here.

I've looked all over the place. She isn't in any of the other rooms... Why can't they just leave me be with my Poopsie?... That dragon, Critch!... Telling me I can't have Poopsie in my bed with me... Telling me she'd see to it that they take her away from me, take her to the pound... But she got her comeuppance, didn't she.

His eyes roaming around. A menacing look.

Poopsie!... You sure she isn't here?

# Dementia

She's not here.

I say she *is*... Where did you hide her?

He's coming in!... Going to the bookcase... Opening the side compartment... Just Glenlivet and glasses, my friend, no Poopsie... He's rushing into the bathroom... Now the bedroom... Opening the closet doors. Can't open the one in the middle.

In here! That's where you're hiding her! Open it! Now!

Can't. No key.

Liar! Open it...

Paul, she isn't here.

****

Jonathan's voice.

Come, let's go. I'll help you look for her.

He takes the man by the arm, leads him out of my room. A look back at me.

That dog's everything to him.

The murder of Charles—it happened while Marlene and I were in Tanzania...

Go back first. That other incident, another intimate body experience, more hurtful—much more hurtful—early in our second year at NYU. Jolene, Charles' girlfriend, that in-your-face Afro, a sunny free spirit, having grown up in a good foster home, bright, had a scholarship to Brooklyn College, graduated

32

summa with a BA in English, was full of life. Taught English at a ghetto middle school, in East New York—I have to teach, she said, do my bit to save their minds from going to waste. Charlene and Winston adored her, almost as much as Charles did. Jolene moving in with Charles—in our new apartment near NYU, three bedrooms, the one we four, the four Charleys, had rented—Marlene then with us too. That day. Jolene and Charles taking a walk. Two men, white, out of nowhere, pulling Jolene and Charles into a dark doorway, knocking Charles unconscious, gagging Jolene, raping her.

\*\*\*\*

Charles asking us to help convince Jolene to go to the Medical Center, Jolene who just sat there, stony, distant. Caroline was firm, made Jolene listen. Caroline, Charles, and I taking her to the Center... Where were Carlo and Marlene?—Ah, yes, visiting his mother and grandparents in Berkeley and her grandparents in Los Angeles... . At the Center the rape procedure—a full medical examination, the taking of a sperm sample, the summoning of the police, rape counseling.

Jolene's eyes were empty when she came back to the waiting room.

\*\*\*\*

Two months later her knowing for certain she was pregnant, full of life in another way. She told Caroline and me, saying she was ashamed to tell Charles, who wasn't, couldn't be, the father. She felt dirty, now totally, wanted to crawl into a corner and die. Caroline, fantastic Caroline, talking at length—How forceful her words!—reminding Jolene how precious she was to Charles, us, Marlene and Carlo, Charlene and Winston, her foster parents. She said Jolene had the strength not to allow defeat, said it much better than in my recollection now. We persuaded her to have an abortion—I'd arrange it, at the Center where I worked. We'd keep it secret. Afterwards Jolene telling us she didn't want to have anything to do with men anymore. Caroline, who had a low opinion of men in general, but who admired Charles, said that some men were alright, that Charles was one of them. Jolene and us then telling Charles about the abortion. He didn't say a word, just held her in a long embrace, nodded at us. But the anger overflowed from his eyes.

Jolene and Charles getting married three years later, having two children, Charlene and Winston—Charlene who became a teacher like her mother—Winston who became a lawyer, my lawyer too...

Carl should call him. Tell him about Nurse and Gloria, He'll know what to do...

\*\*\*\*

Two months after the abortion Charles recognizing one of the rapists in the street, noting his address, following him for days, seeing him together with the other man, finding out their names. Let's kill them, you said... Marlene agreed... Where did the violence come from, welling up in you, taking hold of you, then lingering on subterraneously, until it erupted, full force, those many years later?... Charles looking at me with utter surprise in his eyes, saying no, let the law take care of it. Me hiring that lawyer again. The charges pressed, Charles and Jolene testifying—She didn't want to at first, wanted to be left alone, until Caroline persuaded her—The Medical Center's forensic evidence that the act had not been consensual, had been forced, both men's DNA, the DNA from the sperm sample the Center had taken, also the DNA of the fetus—Caroline had insisted. Ten years prison for both men—Justice prevails now and then, even for African Americans, but so rarely...

Charles successful as a Public Defender, then opening his own practice, defending Brothers accused of theft, car-jacking, robbery, possession, dealing, other crimes—defending also those charged with substance abuse, victims twice over, victims of their skin color and of addiction...

Drug addiction, another cancer, killing both one's body and one's soul... Jo! Why couldn't you protect her?...

A voice from the door, How are you doing?

It's Jonathan... Luckily I'm in the wheelchair—That was close.

Sorry about the Poopsie thing... We found her. She was under Paul's bed all the time... What about you? Would you like to go down to the garden?

Will Gloria be there?

I'm afraid not.

Why?...

Wait! You remember... The tombs... You have to get her out of there...

But you have to go back first. So much to remember, to clear up...

Thank you, Jonathan. Maybe later...

****

Charles defending Brothers. Often false arrests, letters from inmates about beatings or about miscarriage of justice at their trials, false testimony, Charles often reinvestigating, sometimes suing the prison system and police departments. Winning some cases outright but most cases by pleading down, at times way down. Charles White—my other dear friend in those early years—relentless, eagle-eyed, single-minded, anything but schizophrenic—winning a battle now and then, but the war may well be lost, he said, was probably lost from the beginning...

Jolene writing how Charles went to Mississippi to assist a friend, white, just starting as a Public Defender, in the defense of a black man accused of raping a white woman. Charles alerting his friend to flaws in the prosecution's case, and to the means of proving the testimony of a key witness to be false. His friend managing to win, sort of—It was a hung jury... It wasn't a chess game, though. Charles disappeared in Mississippi, was murdered in Mississippi—hanged?—a victim of dead souls— they *had* to have their lynching—raging violence spurning even the guise of law, an intimate body experience from outside the law, more vicious yet—His body never found...

Carl, what about the violence in *you*?...

\*\*\*\*

Charlene never sang again... Jolene continuing to teach, raising young Charlene and Winston, doing it very well. She stayed single. Charles the only man in her life, she said.

Charles who had friends at human rights organizations, who had contacts abroad, who found out what had happened to Caroline.

Caroline. Six foot one, almost as tall as I, statuesque—How powerful the vision still is!—Hair the color of chestnut, cut short, hugging her cheeks, deeply brown eyebrows, deeply brown eyes, broad and straight shoulders, fine features but strong, as if chiseled, startling against the translucence of her skin—Caroline with the long hands, longish neck, somewhat

Modigliani. The Amazon, some called her, which she hated. You should be a model, others said, which she hated even more.

You met her at that party...

\*\*\*\*

The door opening... Don't stand there—sit down!

Edie?

I'm early today, have to leave earlier. I'm chaperoning this afternoon. The girls' class will be taken on an excursion. The teacher needs help with supervising.

The girls?—Ah, yes, Joanna and Joellen.

It's also their birthday today, remember? You wanted to see them.

Carl has forgotten—Not that too!

I'll bring them this evening, around six, for a short visit. That'll leave you time for Gloria afterwards... Here, the gifts I got for them from you. Lego. They like that. They like to build things... Where shall I put them... Here, on the bookcase.

Thank you.

What would you like to do till lunchtime?

Carl doesn't know. What is there to do, here, now? He would like to go back, back to Caroline, even though things turned out badly—Yet so much was beautiful and good...

But it's nice being with Edie, here. Close and warm. She looks good in that yellow outfit. Still slim. Warm blue eyes, lively. Nice white hair... Somewhat like Gloria's...

She brought flowers. Different from the others. Roses, yellow roses. Carl remembers, yellow is her favorite color.

\*\*\*\*

It's my wedding anniversary. I thought we'd first celebrate it together. I brought some candy, the pralines you like. Let's sin.

Not a religious bone in her, but she likes to say, I'm sinning, when she allows herself to indulge in something—New clothes, rich food, sweets.

That praline tastes good... Take another... That's enough... Hand the box to Edie...

You finish them. I'll smoke for a while. I'll stay here by the window...

Fill the pipe... Light it...

That special smile, that broad one, showing her gleaming teeth.

It's coming back...

She and her bridesmaids with those bouquets of yellow roses at her wedding. She with that special smile of hers, radiant. Her long blond hair—glowing—heightening the blue of her eyes...

The strong resemblance to *her* in the photo, so strong now in the memory...

Edie had just turned nineteen when she married, marrying instead of going to college.

He refused to give her away, to attend the wedding. Forbade me to go, but I went. It was Edie's wedding. Bill was an elementary school teacher, not good enough for Edie. Why, she asked me. Having been away at the boarding schools, she didn't understand—she didn't know him as I did. He had wanted her to get a degree in Home Economics or a foreign language, or in something else that was appropriate for a woman, he had said, an education that would prepare her for a man of class...

Is that what *she* did? And then married *him*?... No, don't you remember him saying once she had a degree in Economics, then reminding you again that you had killed her?...

Maybe he would have listened to her, would have been different?... Would things have been different?

He wrote Edie a note, Edwina, you broke my heart.

Bill, gentle, a good mind, well-read, quoting Shakespeare— Edie and he were in the high school drama group together, meeting there for the first time when she was a Freshman, he a Senior, wasn't it?

****

Bill worshiped Edie. They had good years, before things fell apart. Good years with Carlton and Christine, then a few also with Carlton and his wife Belinda—No children, though, Carlton wanted to wait—Carlton, who got the MBA my father wanted for me, who got a job with the oil company, smoothing things over for a while between Edie and him, because he had a Carlton following in his footsteps after all. Mending his heart? Perhaps softening, a little, what was left of a heart? Not much, it turned out—He would have little to do with Edie after Carlton died. Him disinheriting both of us, to the extent that the law allowed. I couldn't have cared less, but it hurt Edie.

Christine. Pretty, pert Christine. Always cheerful—until she married Fred. Fred who fathered Joanna and Joellen, who drank himself blind, who beat Christine, brutally, the little ones too. Carlton, always gentle, like his father, Carlton who loved his sister and the twins, who took a baseball bat to Fred, crippling him for life—Carlton, *his* namesake, my namesake, violence in him too, hidden until it erupted. Sentenced to five years probation—Mitigating circumstances. Then having that heart attack, fatal—left ventricle dysfunction, the autopsy revealed, probably congenital, they said... Inherited, not from *him*—He boasted about his doctors saying he had an unusually strong heart—but maybe from *her*? Was that the real cause, undetected, of her death?...

You're still responsible, he would have said...

****

Christine's divorce—that was good—but then the cancer four years later, so horribly sudden, out of nowhere. You failed to save her...

Belinda moving to Wisconsin, having remarried. Then Bill dying
...

It's still good, Edie said. I have Joanna and Joellen... How strong she is, how resilient!

****

The twins will be alright financially when I'm gone, Edie too—Winston doing my will, a trust thing, doing it even though he's a criminal lawyer, defending Blacks... It's good, how he reminds me of Charles...

Look!

Edie's voice.

I found something on the animal channel, about the Serengeti. Do you feel like watching it?

Okay.

Carl's with it. He's been there. He's prepared for the violence that's a necessary part of the wildlife beauty, prepared for the predators—the lions, the crocodiles... There, the lions after the gazelle... Separating it from the herd... Now the kill...

Jo... Leonard... But that's another wildlife—one that knows the violence of retribution...

Carl must look... There, scenes in the rainy season...

You're aware Carl can't pay attention anymore. He pushes the wheelchair back, then forward again. He's aware his thoughts are wandering, wandering back to the window and then beyond the garden and the trees...

Caroline. You see it all clearly, feel it again. Crystalline. The flashes of light, brilliant, multiple refraction. But also the hardness.

****

Meeting her at that party, towards the end of the fourth semester, a party given by an English prof whose class I was taking, a small class on poetry—I loved poetry. I hated parties, but was I glad later that Carlo had persuaded me to go! Try to have some fun already, he had said. That sublime woman, her imposing beauty—What lucky guy was she with, what fool who didn't stay closely by her side?—Men swarming around her, though not for long, not engaging her it seemed. Her looking, not intimidating, but ill at ease, I thought, which was why I, always uncomfortable at parties, went up to her.

A supremely happy decision. That flicker of amusement in her eyes when I introduced myself, Carlton Carothers, but then the warm, I'm Caroline Carpenter, then the engaged conversation— She told me later I didn't look and act the way she expected a Carlton Carothers to look and act, but that was stupid of her— Caroline straightforward, fine sense of humor—like Carlo's, but drier. That smile, that beautiful, beautiful smile, producing dimples in her cheeks, enslaving me from then on. The conversation flowed easily, about this and that, about shows we both had seen, about Columbia and classes, but mostly about poetry—She too loved poetry, knew a lot about it, more than I—Also her telling me she worked some evenings at a women's shelter—not yet, at that time, signaling the intensity of her commitment to women's causes.

****

Me berating myself after the party for not getting her phone number or address. Not knowing who had brought her to the party—it wasn't one of the poetry classmates. Trying in the days that followed to find her. Remembering her saying she had a room near the campus, but I couldn't find a listing in the campus directory or the phone book. Remembering her saying she was an undergraduate assistant but not mentioning in which department. My lingering for hours all over the campus in front of department buildings, hoping to see her. My contemplating going in and asking for her address or phone number, but changing my mind. They would shield her, correctly so.

Then that day when I ran into her in the library, ran into her sort of literally. Her coming towards me, with five books in her arms, saying, oh, hi!, with a smile that indicated genuine pleasure at seeing me. Reaching for my hand when I extended it. The books falling to the floor. Us both bending down to pick them up, our shoulders touching. The jolt, the rush that went through me. Her saying yes to a cup of coffee. Over coffee her saying she liked it that I was obviously on the shy side, despite seeming to be at ease in the conversation—Oh, Caroline, how could you know that the ease flowed from you? The ease but also the surge of electricity? No contradiction there, not to me— My telling her how I had wanted to find her, how I had kicked myself for not asking her how I could reach her. Her laughing, Well, here we are...

Where are you?

Another voice...

Daydreaming? You have a faraway look in your eyes.

Edie's voice... There—Her lovely smile...

Carl blows her a kiss...

He should keep her company... Didn't she say it's her wedding anniversary?... He really should...

He feels himself drifting away again...

Seeing each other two or three times a week in the months that followed—the end of Spring and then Summer. Drinking much coffee, though not meeting for long each time. That undergraduate assistantship, in the Sociology department, occupied her, also during the summer semester. Being charged with proctoring exams, tutoring fellow undergraduates, other obligations. Being occupied also with the women's shelter, where she volunteered four evenings a week. She didn't talk much about the misery she witnessed there—that came later—but I could sense it weighing on her.

\*\*\*\*

Her earlier years. Her parents dying in an airplane crash when she was three. Living in Florida—Orlando—living there with her aunt, her father's sister, and her uncle until she was nine, then with another aunt, Frieda, her mother's sister, in Chicago. That shadow in Caroline's eyes as she was telling me the reason for the change, telling me the story of her Florida uncle. Him holding her on his lap just a little too tightly, stroking her hair just a little too intimately, then one day putting his hand up her skirt, coming to her room that night, saying, let's play doctor, but quietly, this is just between you and me. Her kneeing him, hard.

She told his wife, her aunt, who called her a lying bitch, who sent her to Aunt Frieda in Chicago.

The years in Chicago were good. Frieda loving and nurturing. But things were tight, Frieda being single, working in a small, privately owned bookstore, sometimes into the evenings, the pay not much. Caroline spending the afternoons after school and some evenings in the bookstore—Frieda didn't want her to be a latchkey kid—Caroline reading and reading—novels, plays, poetry, books on art, increasingly works in sociology, psychology, anthropology.

In the high school years playing basketball, playing Center because of her height. She loved it. It gave her a strong sense of belonging—other than with Frieda—and confidence, a strong sense of purpose. Only when I asked, how, did she tell me her team won the girls' high school championship three years in a row.

**\*\*\*\***

Babysitting, using the money to buy clothes and shoes, to lighten the financial burden on Frieda. In her Junior year— Again that shadow in her eyes as she was telling me—her sitting a two-year old, with seemingly happy parents, but the father groping Caroline one evening while his wife was putting the child to bed, Caroline decking him...

Why did this have to happen to you again? The violation, yet it making you strong and determined—fatally—in the protection of women?...

Offers of basketball scholarships, but accepting a tuition remission offer from Columbia, working in a bookstore the first year, then getting the assistantship. She made just enough money to cover the rent for her room, food, other necessities...

You were in awe of her, even more than of Carlo and Charles ...

**\*\*\*\***

The patience she had with you, with your reluctance to open up, her letting matters drop when you glossed them over, but slowly getting you to drop your guard, to talk about the years before Columbia, the years with him—without him—about learning to turn your back on those years, yet knowing full well how privileged you were. Then talking about your plans, which you had kept to yourself before, the desire that had been growing in you to become a doctor, one who treats cancer. Her saying you seemed to have found the way to yourself... It was mainly you, Caroline, who did it.

Edie and Bill took to her right away, very much so, as I expected, and she to them. She's special, Edie said. Yes, though special doesn't come close to doing justice to the meaning of Caroline. Carlo and Charles took to her as well, as I expected, and she to them. Carlo with that gleam in his eyes when he saw her for the first time—I had asked him and Charles to meet us in the coffee shop, to get to know Caroline—but the gleam disappeared, Charles told me later, when Carlo looked at me looking at her. Charles also saying, You're a lucky dog, don't ever let go of her.

Friendship, warm, open, uncomplicated, liberating.

A measure of freedom also when I got the job at the bookstore, where Caroline had worked. It was my decision to apply, but the power came from her.

You didn't have the strength to wean yourself entirely of his money, but getting the job led to a new beginning, which came two years later, when you entered Med School at NYU, when you got scholarships and loans and then the evening job as an orderly at the Medical Center.

Betraying me once again, he said, with granite in his eyes.

****

You never took Carlo, Charles, or Caroline to meet him—Marlene yes, much later, and Jo—but not the people dear to you then... I still feared him, I guess, still felt the cold hardness. But my new world, the opening world, had also made me be ashamed of him...

And why was it I never tried to kiss Caroline in those months, even though I wanted to desperately? I was afraid I'd step over the line, I guess. The shadows of the funny uncle and the babysitting incident?

Her saying one day, out of the blue, I've never been intimate with a man. You must have had a certain expression on your face because she laughed and said, No, not with a woman either. You told her about Concepcion. She said, We're both virgins, then, though you only half.

Then that evening, two days later, when she took you to her room, that first time. How sparse it was! A nun's cell. A bed, a night-stand, a closet, one table, her typewriter and radio on it, one chair, two prints tacked on the walls—Käthe Kollwitz's *Woman with Dead Child* and Frida Kahlo's *Tree of Hope*. On a tiny stand a small toaster oven—She was allowed to keep food in her landlady's refrigerator. Shower, sink, and toilet shared with other tenants on the same floor.

You were listening to music on the radio—Bach, those fugues!—she sitting on the bed, you on the chair.

\*\*\*\*

The music stopped. The silence, long, tense. She gave you that look, a look that said yes but something else too, something that seemed to indicate defensiveness, a shadow of fear. You felt it rising in you, your protectiveness, your anger, but at the same time your overpowering desire for her, overpowering the anger. She must have seen it in your eyes. She got up, walked towards you. You got up, embraced her. That jolt again, powerful. She must have felt it too. You kissed. Just lips meeting, at first. Then the intimacy of your tongues touching, an electric shock more powerful yet...

I see Carl smiling at himself. He's smiling at the language of his emotions, of his actions, as he recalls, as he immerses himself from here in that time again, being there—No sophistication whatsoever—Or is it a language in the mood, the mode, of a romance novelette?...

I *was* a Romantic. Had no distance on myself...

You didn't dare touch her. She leaned her head against your shoulder, holding it there for a while, then stepped back a little, pulled her sweater out of her slacks—That's what she wore, most of the time, slacks and sweaters or tees—and raised her arms. You trying to pull the sweater up, but her head getting stuck in it. More awkwardness as we undressed each other, searchingly. But it added fierceness to your desire, and you could feel it in her, taking possession of her, the way she took hold of you, embracing you tightly, then pulling you to the bed.

That overwhelming want.

****

You freezing, suddenly. Caroline reaching into the drawer of her night-stand, pulling out a condom. Caroline?! You see, she said, I want it, against my doubts, I want it with you, and I'm not totally from behind the woods. You both then laughing, but it didn't drown the desire, nor did your clumsiness in putting that thing on. Then your fear of hurting her, but she pulled you to herself, tightly, into herself. Yes, she said. She winced, but briefly only. The fever with which we took possession of each other. You don't remember how long the wondrous time was, those engulfing, blissfully transporting moments of making love to Caroline—How poor that expression, *making* love—but you arrived at exhaustion together...

The whir of a helicopter?... Carl's eyes become focused. The Serengeti! Herds fleeing from the noise of the machine, the intruder, above—zebras, gazelles, giraffes, water buffalos, other animals. Elephants, there, but they're standing still, seemingly unconcerned. The vastness of the landscape. Now scenes from the camera below. It's after the rainy season. The rich luminosity, as he remembers it, the greening of the trees, the flowering of the earth. Nice that they show growth only, beauty and peace, no violence...

He can't focus anymore. *Has* to go there again...

\*\*\*\*

Discovering the wonderland of that nun's cell—Wide there the world with Caroline. The intensity with which we explored the joy of being in love, the intensity with which we explored the power of making love, with increasing fierceness of intimacy as time went on, soon freely, overcoming all inhibitions. My body her body, her body mine—I thought.

Her saying no when you asked her to share with you the room in the apartment that Carlo, Charles, and you had found. I'm yours and I'm not, she said. You made it possible for me to know my body intimately, to own it, to give and take freely, to be in possession of myself as a woman, even in the forgetfulness that making love brings with it—Those were her words—How strong the remembrance!—But you also made it possible for me to know intimately, to know much better now, how it must be for a woman *not* to own her body, to be taken only, not to be in possession of herself. I mustn't forget that. I mustn't forget that I as a woman belong to women who don't belong to themselves.

You felt it weighing on you, something heavy, indefinable at the time—hidden in the sense that her words made. You trying to make light of it. We need somebody to cook for us. Her laughing—the dimples deep—as she threw the ashtray at you.

A week later she moved in with you. It was stupid of me, she said. I can be with you *and* do my thing...

\*\*\*\*

Do her thing she did, fighting the cancer that is the dispossession of women, the most pervasive sickness perhaps, it too unleashed by dementia, the bane of humanity—Caroline fighting a war that too may never be won...

The power of thriving in the energy and the intimacy that living with Caroline and with Carlo and Charles brought with it. I had become Carl by then—It was Caroline who first called me by that name. I had become the fourth Charley. It was family, kind of, warm and open, something new for me, exhilarating, also the extended family with Charlene and Winston, and later, in the next apartment, with Marlene and Jolene.

Charles sleeping in the living room on the sofa sleeper—I'm used to it, he said—Caroline and I having one bedroom, Carlo the other, that one next to the living room—Charles now the one to hear the noises of passion and pleasure coming from Carlo's bed. Carlo doing most of the cooking, we others the dishes—He enjoyed it, we enjoyed it—All those pasta meals. Having friends over, Edie and Bill too, Charlene and Winston. Going to shows and exhibits together, once in a while eating out together—not Italian! Thai and Chinese, mostly—being invited by Edie and Bill now and then, by Charlene and Winston. The evenings when we met in the living room. Us listening to music, sometimes Carlo singing along when the radio played operas. More often us talking—shooting the bull, as Carlo put it—me being into it too, increasingly gaining confidence in myself, because of the closeness and the warmth...

\*\*\*\*

Anger, too, ever present, lining the discussions—driving anger that soon hurled you into an abyss. The evenings, increasingly more of them, when Caroline spent hours at the women's shelter. When she was with us—How strong the remembrance again!—her silence at first about what she encountered, then her talking about it, the violence the women suffered, talking about it increasingly more often, speaking with rage flooding her eyes, which made them even more beautiful.

Her once saying, of course men are victims of social norms and expectations too, helpless against the demands made on them, or imprisoned in the definitions of manhood, but why so much brutality, against the children too? And at the women's shelters and refuge houses we see just the tip of the iceberg. Below the surface the cold hardness of thousands and thousands of women in the country who submit to the abuse, the violence, because they don't have the means or the strength to escape, or they hope they can turn things around. And in some other parts of the world it's even worse...

How ominous, now as I recall, her drawing that wider circle of women's abjection...

\*\*\*\*

Carlo and Charles getting into it, no less vehemently, venting *their* anger—The close kinship of their issues with Caroline's. You getting into it too, because you had come to see Caroline's world with her eyes, because you had come to understand fully what was eating at Carlo and Charles, and because they and Caroline, the fellow Charleys, had opened your eyes fully to what was eating at you, insignificant though that was compared to their concerns. Us talking once, you remember, about the will to power, which is sick when it drives people to dominate fellow human beings, to take power away from them, and among the disempowered those who are driven to dominate others in turn, the ones who are or are made to be even more abject—The bicycle-racer syndrome, that's what Marlene called it, later, when she had joined us in the next apartment—The bicycle racer who bends over, humps his back to shield himself against what's above and the wind coming at him, while stepping hard on what's below, to keep himself moving ahead.

The first year at NYU and in the new apartment—Us continuing to do things together and shoot the bull.

Then the violence intruding. Closely, with swift directness, the brutality that came Jolene's way. Indirectly too, causing hard resolve to grow in Caroline. If only she had listened to her professors who encouraged her to pursue graduate study in Sociology! It might have taken her elsewhere, but I would have followed her. I have to work hands on, she said, which is why she was going for an MSW. Her spending more and more time at the shelter, then becoming obsessed with other abuses of women, then in particular with sex trafficking—even preteens, she once said—How well I remember the stony expression on her face.

****

That day when she said, I'm joining a group of people who know ways of rescuing women, women enslaved abroad.

I have to do it, she said...

I'll be back before you know it.

She didn't come back. Death laid his hands on her. Her body, Charles found out, one of five washed up on a shore of the Crimea, another one the body of a young girl, eight, maybe nine years old...

You wanted to go to that Black Sea and kill those who killed them... The raging despair. The helplessness...

The noise from the screen—intruding... Carl's eyes making out, dimly, what's happening... It's clearer now... A group of zebras going to the river, to still their thirst. Something darkly gray lunging at one of them standing aside, exposed—lunging fiercely—a crocodile, its tail lashing the water, the prey grabbed, pulled into the water, to be drowned, then eaten...

\*\*\*\*

*Too* clear!... You see Carl get up from the chair, pace the room... You hear the harshly discordant notes ringing in his ears, atonal chords voiced from the other side, the far side, giving sound to the senselessness that killed Caroline, then Charles—them directly, hands on—then Carlo, killing Carlo by driving him into the fury that drove him into oblivion...

Do you want to go down—meet Gloria?

Edie's voice is distant. Carl's not here yet—Collect yourself!... But this is hard too, being here again... The fog not cleared yet.

Yes, Gloria... You go, now, give yourself more time—An excursion with Joanna and Joellen, didn't you say?...

\*\*\*\*

A smile... A kiss on the cheek...

See you this evening, then.

This evening?...

Carl takes her hand, gives it a squeeze. You're aware he's watching her leave... Tomorrow you pay full attention to her! It's not nice, your being away when she's here...

I want to look outside, see the garden... Gloria—Just look at the garden for a while—the rich luminosity with her there. Think of her, of us in the garden...

Be with her there...

Lunchtime!

Jonathan.

Yes, let's go. I want to be with Gloria.

You can't. I'm very sorry.

What?... Why?

She's staying in the basement now. At least for a while. Maybe I can arrange it, tomorrow, for you to visit her there.

You did it again!... Why does this happen to you?... You must...

Wow! Look at you push that chair! Super!

Jonathan's voice full of surprise.

That's great! You're making progress.

You did push the chair just now, didn't you...

It feels bad, deceiving Jonathan...

****

I *have* made progress. Things are clearer... But I'm not ready yet, not ready to talk to them. So much to recall yet, to put in order...

I'll go down by myself.

Good! Get practice pushing the chair. Here, your sweater, just in case—I'll hang it on the back of the chair... And don't forget your pipe and tobacco.

Down the hall... Push the elevator button... Now inside... It's close in here... A sign, Sing-Along, Monday, 7 p.m. Dining Hall. Come join us!—Not with *your* voice—Remember Carlo's raised eyebrow?—Besides, you don't like being among a crowd... First floor... I don't feel like eating... To the garden!... A threshold here, high—push harder... That did it... Now to my spot, by the red and yellow flowers... Here we are...

Go *there* again!...

\*\*\*\*

The day Carlo brought Marlene home, brought her to stay with him, in our next apartment—near NYU—in our first year there. She was twenty-one, but what a commanding personality already then! That handshake—a powerful grip. I'm Marlene, as in Marlene Dietrich—My mother adored her. The way she pronounced the word, mother. Her English later excellent, but not at first. Vow for wow, sis for this, expressions like, he goes on my nerves, it flushed srough my mind. The r's—You loved it—rrrolling forth from way back, from her throat. Her looks Germanic too. Full cheeks, but the face strong, firm structure. Blond hair, cut short—Later long, because you liked it that way—Marlene!—Intense, incandescent blue eyes. A robust body, five foot eight, solid shape—Her loving to jog, doing it for two hours early in the mornings. A deep voice, like Charles's, but smoky. A big laugh, it too coming from deep down. You soon learned to see her beauty. Not ordinary. Not standard, in the glossy way, according to the dictates of beauty. Extraordinary, hidden to the careless eye—obvious, I thought, when she was animated. Which was most of the time.

We all liked her immediately—you, Caroline, Jolene, Charles, Edie and Bill, Charlene and Winston. A fresh wind, her bluntness, her lack of inhibitions, her impulsiveness. We soon knew her to be warm-hearted, her thoughts to be sharply honest. We didn't mind the foul language she used now and then. It was one of her straightforward ways of responding to a foul world.

Her smoking a lot—Camels. Good for my nerves, she said. Us two having smokes together and chatting, on the balcony or in the backyard. What *did* we talk about? Strange, inconceivable now, how that didn't register.

Her drinking, a lot—together with Carlo.

You thought nothing of it.

****

In time her talking about her family and herself. Her mother, Brigitte, seventeen when the family moved to Los Angeles, Brigitte's parents becoming members of the German expatriate group there during World War Two. Her father teaching art at a Junior college, grateful for having the job. Brigitte at age twenty marrying Franz Maurer, a grandson of German immigrants, Marlene born three years later. Franz imprisoned for being a Fifth Columnist. Brigitte taking Marlene to Germany after the war, wanting to be even further away from Franz, Marlene growing up in Munich. Brigitte working a counter in a department store.

Marlene saying with a wry smile that Brigitte drank, a lot, that Marlene had to take care of her mother a lot. Brigitte had started to drink soon after marrying Franz...

Alcoholism in the blood? The possibility didn't occur to me at the time.

It wouldn't have changed anything. I soon knew she needed it for her art, which she needed to fight a much greater disease.

\*\*\*\*

Marlene soon knowing she wanted to be a painter, was admitted at eighteen to an art school in Munich. Didn't stay there for long. Franz, released from prison and deported, moved in with her mother and her—Brigitte didn't want him around but relented when he begged, saying he had no means yet to make a life for himself. Franz active in a Neo-Nazi group in Munich. Marlene, being fully knowledgeable about what the Nazis had done, confronting her father, standing up to him, being beaten up by him. Brigitte using her savings to buy Marlene an airplane ticket to Los Angeles—later divorcing Franz—Marlene, nineteen, finding refuge with her grandparents, learning from her grandfather, richly, getting an A.A. degree from the college where he still taught, getting a scholarship to study art in New York, on the strength of paintings she had submitted.

\*\*\*\*

Her paintings, the early ones. Raw, but you liked them. Surrealistic, at a once-remove from Expressionist art, not yet, at that time, hyper-realistic, though already fierce strokes, stark colors, already touches of violence. A strong touch of satire. Several of the works—some done earlier in California— depicting grinning men in elegant suits and ties, but wearing high boots as well, the pants' legs stuffed in them, the bodies contorted—elongated here, compressed there—the motifs interlaced with others—In one of the works the background an idyllic landscape—a slightly undulating meadow, light blue, with sheep, all of them white, and a shepherd, also in white, a warm blue sky with cumulus clouds—front right a charcoal alligator, coiled tail, red eyes, outsized teeth, gleaming white, clamping on an outsized dollar bill in blue, front left a cadaverous looking young woman, hair black, wearing a diaphanous red gown, the figure suspended in a tree—the tree's trunk and branches white, the leaves blue—front center a man in a blue suit, white shirt, red tie, and black knee-length boots, the figure humpbacked and dwarfish except for outsized hands, one holding a black bible—An outsized vulture—its feathers red, white, and blue—perched on his head...

What's that noise?... Where am I?... The flowers there... I'm in the garden!... Must have fallen asleep... How long?... That noise... A flock of robins—I think it's robins—lots of them—in that tree to the left. Having come together on their way north— or on their way south? What season *is* it?... Twittering loudly, excitedly. Renewing acquaintances? Making new ones? Chatting about their continuing journey?...

Carlo in love with Marlene. No string of women in his bed anymore, the Bandit tamed.

Bathing in our embrace of Marlene.

Two good years. Family now larger, but equally close and warm. Strong companionship binding us all...

You repressing that indefinable something you sensed underneath, something black, which you eventually knew to be that hard resolve growing in Caroline...

Especially tight the friendship between Caroline and Marlene. Genuine sisterhood.

\*\*\*\*

Marlene boxing me in the shoulder once, saying, Vot a vooman! Vot beauty, vot class, vot head on her shoulders. You be goot to her, *ja*?

Marlene strongly interested in what Caroline was doing, admiring her. Shouting once, voice rife with anger, Men! *Arschlöcher*, so many of sem. Caroline loving Marlene's art, being highly knowledgeable about painting as well—All that reading in the bookstore in Chicago. The discussions of *Woman with Dead Child* and *Tree of Hope,* Marlene saying the art was great but maybe she preferred works that were more overtly political and angrier...

Her own paintings later still political, but covertly, and still angry, then her works showing scenes of suffering—Much later she painted infinite anguish as we see it in *Woman with Dead Child*, but in Marlene's works with anger suffusing the pain...

Marlene spitting fire when she and Carlo returned from California and learned about the rape of Jolene. Storming around in the living room... *Schweinehunde!*... *Unmenschen*... Fock sis world!... Taking Jolene into her arms, holding her tight, saying with a soft, caressing voice, Vy did sis have to happen to *you*?

When Charles identified the men she said, Carl is right, kill sem!...

\*\*\*\*

The anger and pain erupting from Marlene channeled into her art—The emotions wildly diffuse, then composed and transposed into the violent visual...

The day of Caroline's announcement she'd go abroad. Marlene the only one to support Caroline in her decision. Yes, go free sem! Take sem avay from sose bastards! The others joined me in imploring Caroline not to go... I never blamed Marlene—Caroline had made up her mind on her own, as she had always done, strong-willed Caroline.

No letters from her—it has to be secret, she had said—no way of reaching her... The agony of not knowing.

Four months after she left that day when Charles told us what had happened to her. You nodded your head, then collapsed, they said. It's still a blur, that day and the days afterwards—intensified by the pall that had descended on my friends—Remember Jolene crying for days?

Marlene strangely quiet—no outburst—turned in on herself.

It was then that you started to drink. Which led to the involutions that determined your life from then on...

When I drink, which I have been doing all these years, which I do before dinner, I do not do it to forget, I do it not to forget...

****

Carl feels cold... It's Spring—I think. The sun not strong yet... Didn't Jonathan put your sweater... ? Yes, it's there... Nobody around. Get up... Put it on... There, this is better...

More cold that came his way, but also more of the warm... Try to make sense of it all...

The robins, still chattering—The whole tree chirping it seems—A lively scene, magical...

Two months into your heartache that night—Marlene, Carlo, and you had been drinking, you heavily—when Marlene came to your room, sliding into bed with you, embracing you tightly. *Armes Carlchen*, she whispered, poor little Carl. This too a blur, but you remembered it didn't end with the embrace. The next day her acting as if nothing had happened... Years later Carlo told you it had hurt, even though he had understood why Marlene did it, and he hadn't felt betrayed by you.

*You* felt guilty, felt searing guilt. You felt you had deceived both Caroline and Carlo. And you felt Marlene had seduced you into the double betrayal. You soon saw how wrong that was, how deeply unjust to Marlene. You had talked to Charles about it, eagle-eyed Charles, who had set you straight. You don't understand her heart, he had said, its passion, the wide reach of its passion, a profound depth of compassion. Consider the possibility that you—drunk or not—wanted it to happen, that you wanted to let go of Caroline, and Marlene knew it...

****

How is it possible to grieve the person you loved and at the same time let her go? Is it that mourning fills the emptiness, saturates it, empties love into memory?...

Still, you had thought you felt a distance towards Marlene growing in you—Strong the presence still of Caroline, your love for Carlo, neither to be interfered with—But you sensed she knew *that* too. Kissing you on the cheek once and squeezing your hand, which you read as saying, I understand—It's alright. Was it then that you started to feel something else, something vague, subterraneous, a tiny spark, something that later grew into your love for her? You would have dismissed that explanation as preposterous had you suggested it to yourself at that time, but did the emptiness have room after all for more than the emotion of grief, its pressing immediacy?...

Was he no longer a Romantic?...

\*\*\*\*

Soon letting go of Caroline's things, all of them, including *Woman with Dead Child* and *Tree of Hope*. It made you accept her presence as past, and doing it seemed to sharpen the memory of her—the beauty and the forcefulness—to give structure to the image in your mind, to give it full and conclusive shape. It also gave you the strength to return to yourself. Gradually seeking the company of your friends, emerging from your room, Caroline's room, listening to music with them again, shooting the bull again. Being with Edie and Bill at times—Edie had been devastated by Caroline's fate, Bill said.

Not quite family anymore, but you adjusted yourself to what was given to you.

Mainly you immersing yourself in your studies the next two years. Becoming a physician. The image of Caroline sustained you, remembering the power of her being... Something else as well?...

At the end of those two years the dissolution, us going in different directions, Marlene and Carlo to Berkeley, Jolene and Charles—he already a Public Defender by then—into a smaller apartment, you to Johns Hopkins for the internship. After the internship residency at Bellevue, then the appointment there in oncology and cancer surgery. Time flying by. You working hard, up to fifteen hours a day, burying yourself in your work, loving it. No social life, except for now and then, infrequently, seeing Edie and Bill, little Carlton and toddler Christine, also Jolene and Charles, Charlene and Winston. The correspondence with Carlo, rare but warm, about what we were doing, strongly encouraging each other... Marlene never wrote.

How content I thought I felt, living a monk's life as it were, a quiet, mostly solitary life...

A yip?... A nip at my ankle?... It's a dog... A Chihuahua...

Hey, little thing—My ankle taste good?

Poopsie! Come here! Don't bother that man... Sorry about that... You're sitting near the spot where she likes to do her job... Her name's Esmeralda, actually, but she has become Poopsie to me.

Paul—I think Jonathan called him Paul. Has clothes on, his hair's combed. Looks human now.

It's okay... Would another spot do?

Yes... Poopsie, here!... I'm Paul—I don't think we've met.

Carl.

Carl... I guess you think it's funny, me having a dog here, in this place... I need her—need her company.

Man's best friend.

Something like that... Without her I'd be even lonelier here... She's with me all the time. Except in the dining hall. They won't allow me to bring her there, the tight-asses... She's done... Good girl!... Let's go!... Well, so long!...

Carlo writing that Marlene and he had decided to go their separate ways, though not mentioning why. Your guilt feelings again. And something else, it too disquieting...

**** 

That day in the art gallery, an exhibit of paintings by up-and-coming artists. Something had compelled you to go—you didn't know at the time what it was. Near a corner two works, one above the other, each with groups of people. Unmistakable the distortions, the stark colors, the forceful, bold strokes. Aggressive the compositions, the consumption of space—the colors—together with the circulars, lines, and angles—linking the motifs convincingly. This undoubtedly, perhaps less the narrative, what caught the eyes of the selection committee members. The signature on both works, *MM*.

In the upper painting unmistakable the likeness of Carlo—body, hair, especially the eyes and the fire in them. A strong presence, the figure large, three times the size of the men behind him, three of them, troll-like figures in suits, ties, and boots, the colors dark—reds and blacks—the bodies deformed, the faces too, grinning with self-satisfaction, grinning at the sword held aloft in Carlo's right hand.

****

The lower painting with several figures as well. In the foreground a man, gray pants, gray shirt, staring at the beholder, face contorted, mouth open—a cry of pain?—eyes white only—sightless?—standing in a field of daffodils. In the background—slightly behind a group of three men, their shapes, indistinct, in blue with streaks of gray and red—a tall woman in flowing white, grasping a young girl, about nine, by the hand, the girl naked and holding a sapling in the other hand, the little tree dead—leafless, the tiny branches drooping. The woman and the child floating in the air, feet off the ground, the perspective making them seem to recede further into the background, it in red and black. The shock of you recognizing the features of the woman as Caroline's. You looking at the man in the foreground again, only then recognizing him as being in your likeness. Not only the height, the shape of the forehead, the sandy hair. You had been fond of daffodils already then—Caroline liked them, shared with you the fondness for other faint flowers as well...

So different, that painting, from Marlene's other works, and so private...

Behind you a deep, smoky voice. Well, do you like them? The voice unmistakable. Hers, even though the German accent was nearly gone. She looked different—a touch of hardness?—but still beautiful in that special way, perhaps more so...

A voice... a man's voice.

May I join you?

Carl senses annoyance taking hold of him, annoyance at another intrusion into his remembrances.

He recognizes the man. It's Richard—he doesn't know the last name. He sits at Gloria's table...

\*\*\*\*

Maybe he'll let me switch places with him?...

Is a pipe smoker too. Carl saw him once in the garden, with a pipe. Nice looking, kind eyes. Edie would like him. Gloria likes him, Carl remembers. He's gentle, like you, she had said, soft-spoken, thoughtful. A retired pianist, like me... Carl had forgotten Gloria mentioning once before she had been a pianist. It had hurt... Why does your mind play these nasty tricks on you?... She has a piano in her room, come to think of it—didn't play it while I was there... Gloria also said that Richard tends to be absent-minded and is very hard of hearing. A woman at their table said to him once, We need a hearing aid! He responded, We need marmalade? Gloria got angry, she said, when everybody at the table laughed. But Richard laughed with them.

Be polite!

Of course, have a seat, please.

Sweet peas? Where?... I don't understand. What...

No. Sit down.

Oh, okay. Thank you.

Richard smiles, a friendly smile, somewhat shy.

I'm Richard Carter.

Carl Carothers.

****

I've seen you here in the garden a lot this past week, and in the salon, with Gloria Marlowe. I'm a bit jealous of you, you know. You're very fortunate. I like her a lot. So beautiful, in a special way, and what a compelling personality! I love to hear her talk, at lunch and dinner. She has so much to say.

Forget about switching places...

I only met her here, but she is—was—an excellent pianist. Juilliard, and then the world. I went to her concerts several times. I have some of her recordings. Play them a lot.

He knows her better than I do, dammit. Well, not quite—I hope. Or?—No, impossible. No need to be jealous. But why had I not heard of her before I met her here? Because you weren't all that much into the music scene, dummy—Painting yes, but not music performance, other than listening to Charlene, Carlo, Giulia sing and to the radio sometimes.

He's pulled out a pipe. Searching in his pockets. Looking for tobacco? He's muttering. Carl can hear, Where *is* that stuff? Why do I forget things so much?

Carl hears himself saying, Welcome to the fold. Happens to me a lot too. Have some of my tobacco.

Why do you say that? You're not whacko. No more than I am.

No, tobacco—to-bac-co. Here.

Oh, sorry... But thank you, I will.

You watch them fill their pipes, light them.

Richard looks downcast.

She wasn't there, at lunchtime.

\*\*\*\*

You've forgotten, again—drowned the matter of Gloria in your remembrances—which you're trying to collect because of her. Richard doesn't seem to know what happened to her. His absent-mindedness? More likely his hearing loss. People must have talked about Nurse and about Gloria having been taken to the tombs, and he didn't catch it. Should you tell him? No. That would depress him or make him angry. Besides, you're going to do something, and Gloria will be back tomorrow. But you should say something.

Maybe she isn't feeling well today. I'm sure she'll be back tomorrow.

I hope you're right.

You see them smoking, the two geezers, sitting there, thinking of Gloria...

The robins taking off, all of them at once. Carl watches, is captivated. The whoosh, the swarm enlivening the sky, first circling, swooping down and up again, then dissipating into distance...

Her giving you a warm smile, then a hug. You felt a twinge, that something else, disquieting... She saw it in your eyes, she told you later... Us talking, you lamely, constrained—It's been a long time. How have you been?—that kind of stuff. Then a man approaching, putting his arm around her shoulders. Nice looking, kind eyes. Another feeling taking hold of you, constricting—jealousy? Impossible, you said to yourself.

Marlene introducing, Carl, Richard... Yes, he a Richard too... Richard also with a painting in the exhibit. An abstract of a narrow beach-scene viewed from above, from a selective eye, a montage, sunny and warm, of shapes suggesting various shells, lots of them, and driftwood filling the canvas, the colors—pastels and whites—beautifully blended, the composition convincing, particularly strong the interplay of half circles and diagonals.

Telling Marlene and Richard you liked their work very much—You don't remember what you said, but it was genuine, *that* you remember, except that you avoided mentioning your recognition of Carlo and of Caroline and yourself. Then you excusing yourself. Saying good-bye to Marlene—for good, you thought.

Her calling me the next day at the hospital—Carlo told me where you're working, she said. Let's meet.

You were silent for a while, then almost said no. But you felt the pull, yielded to it. You suggested dinner at a restaurant, but she said, No, come to my place, I'll cook something.

Bratwurst and sauerkraut. I haven't forgotten. I disliked sauerkraut—still do—but I paid her a compliment. Liar, she said, I can tell...

She could always tell whether I liked something or not...

\*\*\*\*

She could almost always read my mind...

We had Martinis—I'm ahead of you, she said, I've had one or two already—and a Bordeaux with the meal. Asking me about my work, listening intently. You're a mensch, she said. It's good what you're doing. Then with a faint smile, It's hands on, immediate, even more immediate than what she was doing.

The *was* gave sharp clarity to the awareness of Caroline being of the past, and you felt that twinge again, that pull. But you suppressed it, deflected away from it. You said you really liked the painting of Caroline. It seemed to suggest a new direction in Marlene's work. You didn't mention the intimation of anguish and blindness in the portrayal of you. You saw a flicker of a smile again. You're right, she said, it *is* a new direction, and it's one I'm more comfortable with. But I'm not yet where I want to be. I've not yet achieved the vision I'm seeking...

\*\*\*\*

The vision. It was to be the vision of violence and pain, at first driven by anger and the pain of compassion for the violence and pain suffered by others. Then came the abysmal, infinite pain, the pain of horrible loss together with the pain of overwhelming guilt when she gave birth to a dead son, the pain that consumed her and made infinite her compassion for the violence and pain suffered by others. And in time you learning that seeing and feeling pain made irresistible her desire to drink, and drinking, in turn, gave her the power to express what she saw and felt... the involutions taking yet another turn when the drinking killed the child growing in her...

You wanting to ask about Carlo but not doing it. Her looking at you, once more with a smile. Saying—How well you remember!—It had to end. You'd think it would keep us tied to each other, us chasing the same demons, but it didn't. So I came back here. It's good for me here. I'm learning. Fellow painters, very close, loving friendships.

That loving friendships made you decide to leave. A questioning look in her eyes, to which you replied that you had to go back to work.

Her calling again the next day. Come! We both want it, have wanted it for a long time. I know it. You know it.

You asking, Richard? Her replying, he's a close friend, but just that, a friend. Come!

Why *me*? you asked. She replied, That's why.

That tiny spark, being there from the beginning after the ending of Caroline—or even earlier?—became a powerful flame, a passion that would consume me from then on...

Gloria... Carl will do something. But strong still the remembrance, of the bad and the good. Necessary remembrance... Carl has to stay with it...

****

Marlene and me being there for each other, wanting each other, insatiably, with a fierce possessiveness that was new to me, that I hadn't thought possible—The past absorbed and enriched in the present—Cherishing no less us exploring ideas together—being together evenings and nights or, when I had to work evenings or nights, during the day.

Hearing her deep laugh again and again.

Edie, Bill, and their little ones, Jolene and Charles, Charlene and Winston, they all delighting in our delight in each other.

Visiting Brigitte in Munich. You liked her. Her saying, It's good, Marlene and you.

Visiting Marlene's grandparents, Ursula and Bernhard, in Los Angeles. Their contentment in seeing Marlene happy again.

Looking up Carlo in Berkeley. Him saying, You belong together. He was excited about moving to Italy, to something new for him too.

Now and then getting together with Richard and other artist friends of Marlene's. Their generosity in accepting me as if I were one of them.

****

Marlene's paintings quite different for a while—a short while. Sunny, warm—mainly with yellows, light greens, rose, terra cotta. Abstract landscapes, beach scenes, parks. Also a self-portrait—not abstract—when I asked for one. I loved it, the strong face, the faint smile, the long blond hair—glowing—the intense blue eyes. The way I saw her.

Selling two beach scenes and a park scene. Selling them well.

Marlene's agent saying she had found her style.

Marlene becoming restless, increasingly. Not happy with her art. Absent-minded a lot, also when we made love. Her saying once with a deep frown, My work is shit. It's not where I want to go.

She had been drinking steadily, though in moderation, even with Brigitte and Carlo. You saw no harm in it, had had your own occasional drink—a cocktail or a shot or two of Scotch before dinner. You enjoyed drinking with her. But then she drank more and more, before and after dinner, not because of passion or compassion but because she was angry at herself. You thought you had no right to police her—She was her own person—that it would violate her self-possession, which you cherished so much.

One day the self-portrait was gone. I've burned it, she said. It didn't tell me who I am.

Not showing me what she was working on, asking me not to enter her studio, next to the bedroom. Trashing canvas after canvas. The anger at herself fiercer yet. Not wanting sex, for herself, though insisting on pleasuring me.

****

The evening when I was cutting vegetables—carrots, they were. Her saying, speech slurred, You just came home. Sit down, have a drink. Let *me* do that. Staggering to the counter, tearing the knife from my hand, cutting with drunken force, not noticing I still had my left hand on the carrots, cutting my left index finger to the bone. Crying out as she flung the knife away, *Was hab ich getan, was hab ich getan?* She grabbed my hand and put the bleeding finger in her mouth, caressing the wound with her tongue—Much later she could laugh about it, Fuck, what was I thinking? That I could heal you that way?

The cut severing a nerve—It took half a year for the finger to heal completely and for me to perform surgery again.

She stopped drinking, cold turkey.

She couldn't paint—The canvases blank...

Tanzania. That half a year later. Helping to establish and run the clinic in Dar es Salaam, together with Rodrigo, Pierre, John, and with Tanzanian doctors, Patrice, Rosa, and Mogambo, fighting malaria, TB, AIDS, and cancer. Rodrigo, Pierre, John, and you interns together at Johns Hopkins, staying in touch afterwards. Rodrigo going back to Sao Paulo, then to the jungles of the Amazon, then to the Congo, becoming an expert on malaria—he the one who set it all up with the UN—Pierre going back to Montreal, learning there what was to know about TB—John going back to London, becoming dedicated to treating people with AIDS—a close friend had died of it.

\*\*\*\*

Of course we go, Marlene had said. It's important, perhaps even more important than what you're doing here. Her saying, before I could ask, They have easels, paints, and canvas there, don't they? It'll be good for me too, something else, something new.

Marlene finding her vision in Tanzania, finding the collusion of pain, anger, and compassion—the passion that would claim her from then on. Seeing scenes of misery in Tanzania, so many of them. People suffering from disease, from hunger, from abuse. Misery that drove her to drink again, which drove her to paint the pain.

Giving up smoking—My nerves don't need it anymore, she

said—but continuing to drink, freely yielding to the want when that passion took hold of her.

The success—it was huge—that soon came her way. Exhibits in New York, Chicago, Los Angeles, London, Paris, Berlin, Rome, other cities. Selling works left and right, making a lot of money. Not caring much about the growing fame and the money, but thriving in being at work, the unleashing of energy, spending hours and hours at the easel, covering canvas after canvas.

\*\*\*\*

Us traveling, too, to neighboring countries when I could take two or three days off. Sometimes her going alone. More misery seen, more fierce paintings. South Africa—Apartheid. One of the paintings she did there a scene of a veldt, vast and barren in Marlene's eye, in the foreground a tree limb, leafless, intruding from the right off-canvas, reaching across the canvas, just the limb, arced, on a rope hanging from it a black man hanging, seen in the throes of dying, the vision capturing an instant of a body wildly contorted in its infinitely desperate struggle to hold on to life...

When the letter came from Jolene, telling us what had happened to Charles, the clammy reminder that insanity arcs the world...

Those trips to the Serengeti, several of them, us enjoying being tourists, enjoying times of play. Photo safaris, saturating us with the beauty of the vast wildness... One of the reasons why we had to go back to Tanzania, with Jo...

Later you alone, twice, after they were all gone—Caroline, Charles, Carlo, Marlene, Jo...

Jo being born in the Winter of our second year there—New

Year's Eve—Precious Jo. Marlene and me getting married—her joking, We can't let her grow up being a bastard. How blissful the time, now also the absorbing moments with baby then toddler Jo—moments of care, moments of play...

What happened to the photos we took of Jo then?...

Where are you?...

Richard's voice.

Oh, sorry. I've been thinking of things.

****

Happens to me a lot too. The mind going away, traveling. It's hard coming back.

That friendly smile. And a chuckle.

Maybe we *are* whacko... That was good, wasn't it, tobacco whacko?... Thanks again for the smoke.

Anytime.

His eyes serious now.

Let's hope Gloria will show up for dinner...

Standing there. Then a smile again.

Well, see you around...

Carl watches him as he walks away...

My likeness, my brother...

Gloria... Not yet, not yet...

At the end of the fifth year the termination of the clinic as we knew it. It was to be shut down. No money anymore—the funds had been allocated by the UN, to be paid through various agencies, with the stipulation that the Tanzanian government would take over after five years. They couldn't—The country too poor. Rodrigo flying to New York, pleading with the UN, without success, appealing to various foundations, there too in vain.

Marlene furious—One can't just leave them, she said, leave them helpless against the diseases. So much money being made in the West, and the pigs let the people here die.

*****

A few days later her saying, What if *we* establish a foundation? Put my money to good use? I'll make and sell more paintings...

Marlene! Magnificent Marlene...

Carl feels himself shaking... He should have taken a cab after the party. Or wait until the fog was gone...

The foundation... Leonard on the distant horizon... Not now!...

Knowing that Patrice, Rosa, and Mogambo had become supremely competent and could run the clinic by themselves if supported. How much money would it take? Their salaries, the medicines, the equipment? It turned out to be doable, on a modest scale, with sacrifices, but doable—quite a bit more so after we returned to the States and persuaded others to contribute—Marlene traveling all over the world, putting the arm on people.

You opening a practice—a clinic—together with Phil and Marcus, cancer specialists too. Association with Bellevue for major surgeries. The satisfaction of being effective. More successes than failures. Payment forgiveness when necessary. Working normal hours, though—You wanting to have enough time with Marlene and Jo.

Us buying the brownstone...

\*\*\*\*

The house you were later alone in so many years, living with your ghosts...

But happiness for a good while.

Jo. The joy of play with her, of her questions soon—How come...? Why doesn't one...? Marlene and you reading to her, then her reading on her own. Her wide eyes, those deep hazel eyes, radiant within the blond curls, taking in what the world had to offer her, all of it good, except for a boo-boo now and then, not wanting to go to bed, and such. The joy of seeing her grow, grow so beautifully.

Why are those years—Tanzania and that good while after—mostly vague in your memory even though they saturated you with deep contentment? Was it *because* you were on a constant high? Because the good was continuous, without delineations? Because you felt the bonds between Marlene and Jo, Jo and you, Marlene and you to be one and the same bond? Indistinct as well the times of Jo with her many friends, the times of having them over, laughter filling the house, but so distant and faint now in the memory. A blur also the bloom of the visits with Edie and Bill, Carlton and Christine, Brigitte, Ursula and Bernhard, of Jo unfolding even more brightly... Strange, how hard it is for the mind to hold onto memory of the good uninterrupted...

Maybe just *your* mind?...

\*\*\*\*

Oppressive at first the visits to Charlene and Winston, Jolene, little Charlene and Winston. Charlene no longer singing but she and Winston absorbed with Jolene and the growing children— Charlene recovering her vast sweetness, focusing it on them— Jolene resolute in her efforts to make a new life. Strong the bond between them all. The pain still there but slowly receding. Resilience. They'd be alright, we felt.

The one visit to him. Marlene saying, It's nice that Jo has a grandfather here. His eyes staying hard. Us telling him what we had been doing, were doing—Tanzania, Marlene's art, the foundation, the clinic here. Looking at you he said, Still the bleeding heart, eh? and, She's a commie, has painted you red. I pity the child. Jo asking, Daddy, what does it mean, what that man just said? I don't understand. You replying, It doesn't make sense to me either...

Carl has to give him meaning now, him too, as he sorts things out, one after another...

How do you give meaning to what is deranged?...

\*\*\*\*

Marlene painting and painting, continuing to be highly successful, painting scenes of suffering, painting with anger and compassion, at first African scenes indelible in her mind, then also American scenes—ghetto scenes, Ozark scenes, shelter scenes, scenes of brutality, portraits of people in despair— Misery here too, not as stark as in Africa, but plenty of it, inexhaustible.

Her doubts at times. Her saying once, Why am I doing this? Why are others like me doing it? Our art makes no difference it seems. What's good in being recognized if it doesn't lead to action? The suffering goes on and on. Getting worse. Maybe I should do something else, work hands on, as you do. The look of uncertainty in her eyes when you mentioned the foundation, and again when you said you were confident she wouldn't cease to believe in the possibility—certainly in the need to believe in the possibility—that art has an effect on social conditions, though perhaps not an immediate one. But it's hard, she said, carrying my baggage—I'm still chasing my demons, the demons I share with Carlo. You saying, You wouldn't be the great artist you are without that baggage. Her holding you tight, Carl, what would I do without you?...

How did you manage to do without her, in those years after she was gone?... How did you manage to do without Jo when she was gone too?...

**** 

Carlo coming from Rome to visit us, bringing the Murano vase. Jo took to him right away—He sang *O sole mio* to her. Carlo saying Marlene's art was truly powerful, even more meaningful than what she had done in the earlier years. And the foundation, what a great complement that was to her art! Talking excitedly about Giulia—Obvious his deep commitment to her—and about his immersion in politics—Obvious the intensification of his desire to fight the erosion of an equitable social order and of a social conscience, to fight the politics of dissimulation and sowing discord. Marlene and me relishing his high spirits... Too high?... Close friendship—love, really—ongoing. Us agreeing to come and see Giulia and him in Rome, and then to see Venice.

Going a year later. Jo staying with Edie and Bill, Carlton and Christine—she loved them, loved to be with them for lengthier times.

April in Rome. Giulia stunningly beautiful—pitch-black hair, nearly black eyes, creamy skin. An opera singer, soprano, magnificent voice—We heard her sing Tosca at the opera. She and Carlo performing duets together. Him doing the cooking. Her strongly supporting Carlo's passion. His anger is good, she said, and the energy.

How clearly you remember Giulia saying, I don't like it that he drives so fast, especially fast when he's angry.

Venice in May. That seductive city in her luxurious lagoon.

You felt you had been there before.

The water, everywhere, around her and within her confines, essential to her overpowering beauty, but harmful too—erosion here and there—which increased our desire to be part of her, to possess her, to isolate time—to freeze it—in the moments with her...

****

Marlene enraptured with the mirror I bought for her birthday...

Carl feels himself sitting up. He remembers, May Twelfth her birthday—coming soon. You mustn't forget...

It's gorgeous, she said. That mahogany frame, the superb carvings, what art, the glass embedded in the frame!—Look, the colors, so many, so lively—The richness!...

Marlene getting pregnant in Venice, as we found out months

later.

Marlene briefly seduced into painting scenes of the insistent beauty of Venice—the imposing beauty that endured—but soon giving up, not liking what she saw on the canvas. It's not for me, she said. Can't find the passion I need. Have to find it elsewhere.

Her drinking heavily again when we returned home. She didn't know she was with child, had often missed her days before.

She stopped drinking when she knew, but it was too late. Erosion had taken place. In the seventh month the second heart in her stopped beating...

Marlene sitting in a corner of the hospital room, legs folded, drawn in, body and head bent over deeply, her arms cradling the dead, barely visible little thing in her lap. You didn't hear a sound...

****

Still here?... Deep into your thoughts?

Jonathan.

It's getting colder out here. Maybe you should button the sweater... Here, a flask—some of your Glenlivet. It's yardarm time for you.

His concern for me. Because I took care of his father those years ago?... You're like a father to me, he once said... It's not only that. He's a mensch, Marlene would say.

I'm fine. Thank you.

Alright then.

He's hesitating...

I just saw Gloria. I'm to tell you she'll be back soon. But don't raise your hopes. Things are still complicated.

He doesn't know, of course... *I* know she'll be back—As soon as everything's cleared up in my mind...

Have a sip of Scotch...

He's giving me that smile of his. Now he's leaving.

Jo, nine-year old Jo, distraught herself—she had understood what had happened—but hiding her own pain in the depth and tenderness of her compassion for us. Motherly almost her loving compassion for her mother. Coming into bed with us, enfolding Marlene with her arms, holding her tight. It'll be alright, she murmured. The penetrating simplicity.

Giving *me* the little silver vase—simple, delicate...

****

Understanding—accepting—Marlene's occasional heavy drinking again, having understood her mother's habit of drinking all along—I know you need it, Mom, she had said once, earlier, you need it for your work... Jo knowing her mother needed it now more than ever.

Marlene never liberated herself from the guilt and the grief. Which is why her work became more powerful yet, her compassion for people suffering violence and pain having become all-consuming. The energy! Fed by her renewed passion, fiercer than ever before. Renewal also of our passion

*82*

for each other, despite the guilt and the grief—because of it?—Being there for each other, intimate friendship, giving and taking. True the saying, true in so many ways, that pain and pleasure may collude.

Our shared delight in watching Jo master the preteens. Little tragedies—large in her eyes—but soon overcome. Becoming conscious of her body, discovering the existence of sex, like her friends discovering it awkwardly. Asking us about it but not wanting to know all that well—Ick! she once said. You two did *that*? Doing well at school, growing trim and tall, supple and agile—Watching her do well at gymnastics and other sports—our little gazelle...

Carlo speeding to his death...

\*\*\*\*

Those two paintings of car crashes. The violent images of flying crushed metal filling the canvas. Cold metallic silver on ferociously applied blacks and reds, some grays, browns and purples—crushing...

Being there for Jo as she embraced the world with loss of innocence about humankind. Her mother's art opening her eyes to suffering, her taking in, comprehending, the poverty, the violence, the helplessness, around her and beyond. Her father's work—Asking me about it, insisting once on coming to the hospital—learning about *that* pain and dying as well.

Seeing more misery when she went with us to Tanzania, but being enthralled with the Serengeti—with the beauty of the landscape, the elephants, the water buffalos, the zebras—the gazelles.

Reluctantly comprehending the necessity of violence lacing the beauty.

Being excited about the foundation, the Tanzania Clinic Foundation, what it was doing. I'll work for it some day, she said.

Marlene having the break-down. Too much, the energy she spent at her work, and the drinking. The immune system shot.

It's been eating me up, she said, inside and outside. Like a cancer. It's killing me...

*It* didn't kill her.

****

Marlene recovering—Us taking care of her... Jo's solicitude, her spending after school hours and hours with her mother, seeing to it that she ate, urging her to get well again so that she would paint again, to take care of the foundation again.

Marlene going back to work, recovering the power of her art. More success.

****

Jo growing more beautiful yet. Marlene and me watching her struggle with the teens. The hormones hyperactive, her using foul language—language that was fouler even than Marlene's. Bitches, some of her classmates, fuck their ass-holes. The world is dog shit. Piss on it! Insisting on getting the right make of jeans, the right make of shoes, the tees that were in. Utter sweetness at other times. Continuing to do well at school, at sports. Having friends over, boys, increasingly. Growing to like boys. She didn't tell, we never asked—Her life was her own. Crying her eyes out when she felt betrayed by one of the twerps.

*84*

Us consoling her—There would be others... Jo writing poetry, but not showing it to us... So beautifully normal, then, her life.

Discovering carpentry, loving it, spending hours at it. She turned the basement into her workshop. Becoming accomplished at carpentry—It's like what you're doing, Mom, and a bit like writing. Marlene saying, Maybe it's even better—it's not only hands on, it's art that's a closely intimate part of our everyday life, for us to touch—to feel as well as to see—the forms liberated from the wood that came from the forests—to be one with the forms.

Apprenticing with a carpenter who had done some work for us, Jo thriving—getting her own shop, doing repairs, selling pieces of furniture, increasingly more. Also getting an A.A. degree—Like you did, Mom. Then also working in the New York City office, the headquarters, of the Tanzania Clinic Foundation. Learning the ropes, doing it very well...

Time flying by, the good uninterrupted...

Marlene appointing Jo, twenty-four, director of the foundation. No, Jo had said, it's nepotism. It's your efficiency, Marlene had replied, and whom can I trust more than you?

Jo highly successful in raising money, traveling all over the world. Her infectious enthusiasm...

Leonard Lowell among the guests at Jo's twenty-fifth birthday party, a New Year's Eve party. They had met at a fund-raiser. He had been very attentive to Jo, she said. Had wanted to know all about her. She had felt the electricity between them. And he had shown a strong interest in the foundation—how it was run—in Marlene's fame, in my work, the success of the clinic.

Jo deeply in love.

A month later she had hired him as director of the foundation's legal affairs.

****

You have to admit you liked him at first. He had charm, was smart, well-read, very good looking, tall and muscular, had rowed for Yale. Graduated from Yale at age twenty-one, from Harvard Law School at twenty-five, had been working for three years in a corporate law firm. That didn't impress you—What impressed you was that he took the job at the foundation with a pay cut.

His heart's in the right place, Jo said.

You agreed...

The bitter twist. The gods of the Greek laughing...

Marlene disliked him right away. I don't trust him, she said to me. Something in his eyes. Seems false to me. Flashing that smile too often. He strikes me as being a suit through and through. Doesn't gel with working for the foundation.

Managing to hide her misgivings from Jo. I may be wrong, she said. I should trust her instincts. Let's wait and see.

She wasn't given the time to wait and see. You weren't given more time with her. Two months after Jo's birthday that party at Leonard's. Jo and Leonard announcing they'd get married. Marlene drinking—The apprehension in her eyes—then saying, I want to go home...

You drove the car. The fog. The road slippery. A truck suddenly looming, hurtling at us from the left, ramming us into another truck to the right. You unexplainably untouched. The right side of the car crushed to a pulp... A lumpy form of crushed metal laced with blood... Marlene and crushed metal as if they were one...

**** 

Mister Carothers! Enjoying the garden, I see.

What?... Not *now*!... You need to be by yourself...

It's a nurse—-Clarice, I remember her name!—pushing a wheelchair towards me... I know that man sitting in it. It's him, the one at my table who sits next to the woman across me—the imminent departure guy.

He's giving me a smile, a toothless smile... He's gumming some words I can't make out...

As the nurse is pushing him by you he still smiles, and—are you mistaken? No, you see it clearly—he's giving you the finger...

You mustn't tear yourself up like that, Dad. It was an accident, not your fault.

We were tight, for a year—there for each other—after Marlene was gone. Jo making the bookcase for me. Remember, she said, I drew the design before she died. She loved it.

Jo then spending all of her time at the foundation...

She would have been a great artist in wood, liberating forms of beauty...

Her moving in with Leonard...

Things happening fast from then on.

****

That evening at their apartment. Many guests. On the bathroom counter the coke, for all to help themselves. You confronting Jo and Leonard. It's not a good idea, the dope. Him grinning, It's recreational. It's nice to get a kick from a snort now and then. Oh Dad, she said, everybody does it. There's no harm in it when you do it only occasionally.

You should have done something then and there, but you couldn't. Paralysis? Evasion? Perhaps, you thought, you were being a fuddy-duddy.

We want to get married New Year's Eve, on my birthday, she said. Do you think it's too soon after Mom dying?

You should have told her what her mother had said, should have mentioned your own growing doubts about the man. But you didn't. The risk of driving your daughter away from you. No matter, you should have done it. Something might have warned her, might have opened her eyes.

Give yourself more time, you said. Not because of Mom. Get to know him better.

The slight frown. What's more to know? He's terrific. Does a wonderful job at the foundation. Everybody likes him. I love him. He loves me.

You felt cheap for even thinking of asking her if he knew she was her mother's sole heir.

****

The wedding taking place in our home that New Year's Eve, Jo's twenty-sixth birthday. Leonard's friends there, lots of them. Not his parents—We're estranged, he had once said. Charlene and Winston, Jolene, her Charlene and Winston, Edie, Bill, Carlton, Christine. Edie and Bill had met Leonard once before. You remember the guarded look in Edie's eyes.

Not seeing Jo for quite a while, though her calling once a week, saying she was blissfully happy. How was I doing, and such.

Then her coming to the house one evening. The pink in the whites of her eyes. Are you still doing coke? you asked. Only now and then, she replied. Nothing to worry about. All's well.

Only phone calls for the next months, through the Summer and the Fall, Jo assuring you everything was just fine...

Why did you believe her?... Why didn't you insist on seeing her?... Why didn't she tell you?...

That day, a day in late November, when she came with a suitcase. Crying bitterly. He's been cheating on me, again and again. Did it already on our honeymoon.

The needle marks. Heroin? you asked. I need it, she replied. Makes me forget. He makes love to me—is nice to me— only when he's high on heroin. He said, Try it, you'll like it.

She promised to leave him, to go into rehab.

Two days later she was gone. She had left a note, I need him. I can't live without him.

You going to the police. We can't help you, they said. She has to come to us and testify.

# Dementia

\*\*\*\*

You trying to call her. Got the machine. No call back.

You going to their place. Go away, he said. She doesn't want to see you. Don't stick your nose into business that's not yours.

She called on New Year's Eve, her twenty-seventh birthday. The voice desperate, her speech inarticulate. It's our first anniversary and he isn't here with me... He was going to get some fresh ass, he said... Oh, Daddy, what shall I do, what shall I do?... I want him so badly.

I'll be right over, you said. Wait for me. Stay away from that stuff. Wait! It'll be alright.

Forty-five minutes! The distance. The traffic. Forty-five minutes an eon when you have to be there right away.

The police were there when you arrived. They let you in when you identified yourself.

The heroin paraphernalia on the coffee table, the large one— She had made it when Marlene was still with us.

In the bedroom her body, the head not a head—half a head, that a bloody, jagged pulp... The blood on the wall... The teeth.

The neighbors downstairs had heard crying and moaning, then a gunshot. Had called the police.

Leonard showing up... What a mess, he said.

The police detective pulling you aside. We'll drive you home. I don't like what I see in your eyes.

****

Leonard calling you the next day... Later you were grateful to him for that—for letting you overcome your paralysis—for giving you the opportunity of letting vengeance edge your despair.

He sounded high. I need you to come over, he said. I'm going to buy an apartment in town—I can afford it now—and I want to get rid of her things. Come and select what you want to keep. The coffee table, for one...

The paraphernalia on the coffee table. The burner still on. He must have helped himself again.

Bringing a bottle of Glenlivet from the bar, pouring some into a glass, spilling a lot of it, putting the bottle on the coffee table.

You taking the bottle and hitting the side of his head with it, very hard, drawing blood, rendering him unconscious. You cooking some more of that stuff, injecting it into him, twice repeating the procedure. You hitting a spot on the rim of the coffee table with the bottle, making a dent, wiping some of his blood on the indentation, arranging his body on the floor so that the cracked part of his head rested on the bloodied spot on the rim.

****

The police calling me the next day, to tell me he had been heavily drugged and had fallen on the coffee table. The autopsy wasn't conclusive, couldn't tell them what had killed him, the drug or the fall... I think they didn't care...

Yoohoo!... Yoohoo!...

A woman coming towards me. Tall, skinny... No! It's the one from my table—the witch—she who plays footsies... I can't deal with that now...

She looks different today—it's the way she's dressed—All those colors, the big yellow hat. And heavily made up—Thick rouge, deep blue eye shadow, thick mascara...

Carl! I thought it was you. What a nice surprise!

A chirpy voice.

Pointing at the bench.

I think I'll sit down here. Take a load off my feet.

You can't say, Get away from me, can you.

Please, have a seat.

She does.

We can finally have a chat... What a nice day!... A bit chilly, though... The garden's so pretty... Not too many people around... I'm glad I've run into you. And you look like you could do with some company too... I'm Ricarda, by the way— You've probably forgotten my name. Here's my chance to talk to you. You don't say much at the table.

She gives me a long look.

But then there are those who don't want company, or those who think they don't.

She's looking at the red flowers.

****

One must look pain in the eye. But you know that... Lots of people here who have to cope with loss. I lost my husband twelve years ago. Two years later Jim. my son, died too—was only twenty-seven when he died—A blood clot after breaking a leg... So I'm alone now... There's a lot of loneliness around here... But it's no good to brood, you know. Forget about the past, I say. Look to the future. One has to be resilient... It's not easy, though...

She's looking at me again.

On top of that the doctors here say I'm a bit bonkers. Didn't say it like that, but that's what they meant. Can you believe it?

She's smiling, a warm smile.

I chatter a lot... But *you*, you really don't talk much, do you.

She's shrugging her shoulders.

You try to make yourself look attractive, but that's hard when you're a dog.

You're not...

Oh yes I am. There's no kidding myself. But what can you do?

Now smiling again.

I wanted to come on to you—Never give up, I say—until it became obvious that you have that thing with Gloria Marlowe. She's precious. I wouldn't dream of interfering... I hope the two of you can soon sit at the same table.

She knows about that?... How?... Does she know about the tombs?

A serious look in her eyes.

I can't believe they took her to the tombs.

Ah.

It wasn't her who killed Critch... No way she could be violent... Now *I*, I could be. You and I, we're not that far apart, you know.

The look intent.

It's good that you're going to talk to them. It may mean that I won't be seeing you again. But who knows, right?

She's looking at her watch.

Five already?... Time to go... Dinnertime soon... Well, I'm off... I really enjoyed this...

Carl hears clicking noises as she walks away. She's wearing high heels, gold-colored. He didn't hear the clicking when she came...

The way she's dressed. A firebird. The gold shoes, the red blouse, the chiffon skirt yellow and orange, down do the ankles, the blue and red cape down to the waist, the gold necklace, the large gold hoops in her ears, the purple and green scarf, the big yellow straw hat... A lively scene, magical...

The harsh notes from the other side seem to be gone—No longer those sounds ringing in your ears—the fugue of futility. The fog cleared away...

Time to go back in... Push... It seems to be easier now... Over that hump... To the elevator... The button, push it... Inside... That sign again—Sing-Along... The button for the fourth floor... Up... The hall... People... An open door. The man in the room, watching TV, you know him. It's Peter, with the incontinence problem. You promised to visit him, to have a chat with him. That may not happen, the way things are now... Push on!... That's Jonathan there.

****

Jonathan!

Carl!—Pushed yourself all the way again? That's really neat, you know...

I'm ready to talk to him about Gloria, but later. And I want to be ready for Edie and the twins.

I have a favor to ask.

Shoot!

Could I have dinner in my room today?

Of course. I'll see to it.

Another favor. Could you come to my room around seven?

Will do. What's it about?

I'll tell you then.

Sounds mysterious... Seven? But that's when Edie and her granddaughters will be visiting you. She told me it's the girls' birthday.

They come at six, for a short while.

He's smiling broadly.

You remember!... You're having a good day today—a very good day.

Perhaps... Till later, then!

I'll be there.

\*\*\*\*

Push on... Your door... Open it... Go in... Get out of the wheelchair—up!... To the bookcase!—Jo's bookcase... The bottle and a glass... Put them on that coffee table there—one of Jo's tables... Open the bottle... Pour!... Sit down on the easy chair here—one of Marlene's chairs... A sip... Another...

Raising the glass to her in the photo, to her who's far away, but no longer outside... To him too? What the hell, why not... To the sarong, to *her* again... To the Murano vase—to Carlo, Charles, Caroline... To Jo in the photo... And the silver vase... To Marlene in the photo... To the painting there... The other one too... The mirror...

The door... Into the wheelchair!... It's Consuelo, with a cart, a tray on it—your dinner...

Good evening, Mister Carothers.

Consuelo. Good evening.

Follow her into the bedroom, to the little table... Take the glass with you... Can you push the wheelchair with one hand?... Yes.

Thank you.

*De nada*. Enjoy your meal!

**** 

The light of the setting sun... Gloria... The view again... The trees, the bushes, the flowers... I feel like eating now... Lift the lid off your plate!... Lamb, mashed potatoes, asparagus... Tasty... You *are* enjoying this... What's for dessert? Flan—I like Flan... That's good too... Get out the pipe, the tobacco... The whacko tobacco... Fill the pipe... Put the match to it... Finish the Scotch... Look outside...

The trips you took, and the pictures, the first trip a year after Jo was gone. To Tanzania. Where Marlene found her art, where Jo was born, and the foundation. Then other countries, one every year, one again to Tanzania. The grace of the lands, of their people. The cancers you saw, spreading—often under the surface—dispossession, abjection... The photos you took to mirror the images of beauty and violence burnt into your mind—apparitions, again and again, of Marlene, of Jo, of Caroline, Charles, and Carlo...

Twice to Brunei. No photos there, just imagination...

Your work, the cancer clinic and the foundation—They were your life from then on. It was good—for a while. Accomplishments in the clinic, some failures—Christine, among others—the foundation running smoothly, no less when Edie took over, after Bill died. You being busy, up to fifteen hours a day, as in those years before Marlene came to you. Wanting to work hard because it was hard being alone in the house. The feeling of loneliness even though they came to see you—Edie, Bill, Carlton, Christine, then just Edie and Bill, then just Edie. Charlene and Winston were gone, but Jolene came, and young Charlene and young Winston...

Should I call Winston now?... Do it tomorrow morning—hear first what Jonathan has to say...

\*\*\*\*

Still, the loneliness. They had their own lives to live.

Then things happening to your mind, you now know. Not just forgetting things, but not being able to forget things—the images still burning in your mind, burning intensely...

Then *this* place... Gloria... Nurse... Beauty and violence... Passion...

Carl?

Edie's voice.

In here!

Turn the chair around.

Two girls running towards me. Joanna and Joellen... Which is which?—I can't tell them apart... A hug from each of them...

In unison, Carl! It's good to see you.

I need help.

Edie smiling.

The one with her hair parted in the middle is Joellen.

Both of them giggling.

You'll know from now on.

That from Joellen.

What if I part *my* hair in the middle?

Joanna. Mischief in her eyes.

Then I'll call both of you Jo.

Both giggling again.

****

Let's go to the other room. How about you two pushing me?

They do...

Here we are... Catch the girls' eyes...

Today's special, isn't it. Your ninth birthday... Well, here goes, Happy birthday to you. Happy birthday to you. Happy birthday to you, Joanna Joellen. Happy birthday to you... That was terrible wasn't it? I shouldn't sing—not with *my* voice.

They're laughing... An expectant look in their eyes.

See those packages on the bookcase? They're for you.

Joanna going to the bookcase... Reaching for the packages... She stops... She's taking the silver vase in her hand.

Out-a-sight!

Joanna, I think you should put that back.

Edie's voice a bit stern.

It's alright... It *is* quite something, isn't it... I have an idea. We'll have Grandma look for two just like that, or very similar, for you and Joellen to have.

Their smiles bright.

Edie raising a hand.

I don't know... I'll try...

In unison, It's okay.

Joanna taking the packages... Putting one each on a coffee table... Both kneeling down... Tearing at the wrapping paper...

\*\*\*\*

In unison, Lego!—Cool!

Again together, Thank you, Carl!

Opening the boxes... They're starting to put pieces together... Let them—There's time... That melody in your ear, an old melody—Something about doubling one's pleasure... Pleasure... No pain... Gloria... Last night... Your mind wandering...

Time to go!

Edie... She's helping the girls put the Lego pieces in the boxes...

Can't tell her about Gloria... Tomorrow...

She's giving you a hug.

See you tomorrow!

Hugs from the girls too... And kisses... They're at the door... Turning around.

In unison, Bye, Carl! Thanks again.

Laters, alligators!

They're giggling... Now they're gone... Their voices in the hall, and Edie's... Getting faint... Fainter... Now inaudible...

I'm here!

Jonathan.

Get out of the wheelchair... Walk towards him... There... His eyes opening wide.

****

Carl! Now you walk!... That's fantastic! You're really having a good day today.

I have a confession to make. Two, actually. I've been able to walk for some time... I feel bad for having kept it from you...

You're a sly one, aren't you. No matter. The main thing is you can walk...

I've been walking to Gloria's room...

Oho!

... these past evenings. I hope you understand that I didn't want anybody to know I can do that.

You could have told *me*. Now, others on the staff here, that's another kettle of fish.

That brings me to my second confession. It was I who killed Nurse Martha.

He's giving me a long look. Then a smile.

That's a good one... No way... You and violence?

\*\*\*\*

She came to Gloria's room last night while I was there. She said she'd tell on me—my being there and lying about not being able to walk. I couldn't let her tell about my being there. I was afraid it would be the end of Gloria and me. So I pushed her out the window—Strange how silently she went. The surprise, I guess... I didn't think they'd hold Gloria responsible. She had nothing to do with it. She was asleep through the whole thing. You have to let her come up from the tombs... I know it's now really the end of Gloria and me... Funny, isn't it, how things can turn out?

A long look at me again, a longer one.

That's quite a story... What if it's true?... Did you *have* to...? I suppose... The fog you're in at times... Though the mind's sharp today, isn't it... I have to sort things out here. They're quite complicated... Let's see...

His brow's furrowed... Now a smile.

You would like to be with Gloria, right?

Yes!... But...

There *is* a way. Because there's a catch.

A catch.

The law has no evidence against her, other than a flimsy circumstantial one. No motive, no means. They won't prosecute her. But—and that's the first part of the catch—the administration here will not let her leave the tombs, not for a long while anyway, maybe never. Their thinking will be, what if she did it? She might harm somebody else. So they'll keep her there, for safety reasons.

But she didn't...

\*\*\*\*

Doesn't matter... The solution is to get *you* into the tombs... You'll have to tell your story... Now, if the police were to believe you—accept your confession—it wouldn't be the tombs for you, it would be an institution for the criminally insane.

So why do you...

But they *won't* believe you. There's no evidence to support your confession. Your lawyer—You have a lawyer, don't you?—will find that out on discovery. He'll also have *our* testimony—that of the doctors here and the staff—that you can't walk and are very weak, that you couldn't have done it.

But you...

It's going to be my story too. And we'll remind them that you're very close to Gloria, that you've often been seen with her, in the garden or the salon. They'll think you made the confession to protect her. Which will be the truth, except that you did commit the crime.

But how does...?

Here's the second part of the catch. The administration will put you into the tombs, for the same reason as with Gloria. Don't take any risks, they'll argue.

But we'll both be locked up.

Why is he smiling so broadly?

I'll get a transfer to the basement. I'll make sure you'll see each other a lot, in the garden there and in the salon, have your meals together. With me officially supervising.

Is he serious?... Yes, he *is*!... Jonathan!...

\*\*\*\*

Does the garden have bushes, with red flowers and yellow ones?

If not we'll plant some.

Edie? Can she and the twins visit us?

Of course.

Peter? Paul and Poopsie? Richard? Ricarda?

Why not.

Can Gloria have her piano?

Already done.

I want to talk to the doctors about her cancer. I know of new methods they may wish to try out.

They'll listen to you.

What about evenings?... Can I...?

I'll give you both the keys to your rooms.
...

What if they don't transfer him?